TIGHT

Also by Torrey Maldonado

Secret Saturdays

TORREY MALDONADO

 Nancy Paulsen Books

NANCY PAULSEN BOOKS
an imprint of Penguin Random House LLC
375 Hudson Street
New York, NY 10014

Library of Congress Cataloging-in-Publication Data
Names: Maldonado, Torrey, author.
Title: Tight / Torrey Maldonado.
Description: New York, NY : Nancy Paulsen Books, [2018]
Summary: After his quick-tempered father gets in a fight and is sent back to jail, sixth-grader
Bryan, known for being quiet and thoughtful, snaps and follows new friend Mike into trouble.
Identifiers: LCCN 2018007927 | ISBN 9781524740559 (hardback) | ISBN 9781524740566 (ebook)
Subjects: | CYAC: Conduct of life—Fiction. | Inner cities—Fiction. | Family life—Brooklyn (New
York, N.Y.)—Fiction. | Friendship—Fiction. | African Americans—Fiction. | Brooklyn (New York,
N.Y.)—Fiction. | BISAC: JUVENILE FICTION / Boys & Men. | JUVENILE FICTION / People & Places
/ United States / African American. | JUVENILE FICTION / Social Issues / Friendship.
Classification: LCC PZ7.M2927 Tig 2018 | DDC [Fic]—dc23
LC record available at https://lccn.loc.gov/2018007927

Printed in the United States of America.
ISBN 9781524740559
1 3 5 7 9 10 8 6 4 2

Edited by Nancy Paulsen.
Design by Marikka Tamura.
Text set in Diverda Serif Com.

A12006 879684

For the two who help make my life A.R.T.,
the "A" and "R" to my "T": Ava and Rachel

CHAPTER 1

I'm chilling at the community center where Ma works. She's cool with her boss and coworkers, so they're cool with me and my sister, Ava, being at Ma's job after school.

Usually, Ava chills for minutes. Me? Hours. I don't know why Ava doesn't hang longer. Maybe she's too busy with her ninth-grade life. But me? I like doing office things, like Ma: reading, being quiet, and chilling for forever. For example, about a month back, I found this empty spot at Ma's job and asked her if I could use it as my pretend-office. She asked her boss and she told Ma, "Sure. We also have a spare desk-chair and some other supplies Bryan can use."

So, right now, I'm doing homework in my office, but this kid named Mike is at Ma's desk and I'm distracted spying on him.

He's a year older than me and about two inches taller. He rocks a sweater like mine, but his kicks are newer and more popular. He has hair like me, Afro-type if we grew it out. Mine's grown out a little since I need a cut. He just got one.

Now he's alone, but I've seen him with his mom here, two or three times.

I didn't think twice about Mike at first because a lot of kids and their parents come through here. Then I saw him at my school, hanging with seventh graders. He didn't do his sixth grade in my school. So, why'd he transfer for his seventh grade? I asked Ma, and she said his family was in the Bronx and she helped them get an apartment here in Brooklyn in our projects.

In school, me and Mike nod what's up but don't hang. I see him around the neighborhood too and at the handball courts near us. Then the other day I saw him talking to my pops. I didn't get why Pa was so friendly to him. And I don't get why Mike is here now, talking to Ma.

I squint at them.

"Did Mike just call Ma 'Ma'?" I ask Ava, who is in my office looking at my homework on my clipboard.

Ava stares from the clipboard at him and shrugs. "Who cares? Almost anyone younger than her calls her Ma."

That's true. Ma helps lots of people and they love her. But I don't like this kid Mike calling her Ma right now.

I ask Ava, "Why's he playing her so close?"

Ava goes back to reading the clipboard, but I can't look away.

Mike stares at Ma like she's his mom for real and gives her a hug.

Yo! He *better* let go of my moms.

Ava interrupts me and points at different spots on my clipboard. "You spelled some stuff wrong."

"What? Where?" Nothing should be wrong because I checked it twice like Ma says to do. I look where she points.

Ugh! She's right. I hate when she's right.

I grab a pencil, take the clipboard, and fix my mistakes.

By the time I look up again, Mike's about to leave. He yells, "Bye, Ma!"

I turn to Ava. "*He* just called her *Ma* again!"

She rolls her eyes. "Because he's probably her real son. Unlike you."

Here she goes again, cracking that stupid joke she's been cracking since I was in day care, telling me Ma and Pa found me in a trash can.

Back then, I believed her since me and Ava have different complexions. Hers is chocolate brown. I'm a lighter caramel.

The first time she said it, I ran to Ma and she showed me our birth certificates. Ava got punished but she never stopped joking I wasn't her brother—like right now—and for some reason it still bothers me.

"Well, I wish Mike was my real brother," she continues. "He's no momma's boy like you."

My whole head burns like I have a fever. I want to cut on her so hard. But only weak disses come to mind. I finally growl, "Big Head."

"Oooh, *Big Head*. Ouch. I can't wait until Mike comes to eat."

"Eat?"

"What you think? He calls Ma *Ma* and he won't come eat soon? You know anyone who calls Ma *Ma* ends up eating with us. You saw how she hugged him."

Ma sneaks up on us. "What is going on with you two?"

We shut up.

"You both were going at it. Now you're quiet?"

"Bryan's mad because you hugged Mike."

Ma makes a face like I'm her baby and I have nothing to worry about. "Come here."

I go over and she hugs me.

"You don't have to worry about Mike. You'll see tomorrow night. He's coming for dinner."

CHAPTER 2

When I get back from school the next day, Ma tries handing me what looks like a grocery list. I U-turn to bounce.

"Bryan," she calls me back. "Here. I need you to go to Hector's."

I sigh, turn around, and take her grocery list as thoughts fly through my head.

I hope there's no note for the bodega's owner.

I hope there's no note for the bodega's owner.

Ugh! There's a note for him.

Why do I have to get groceries with a note and not real money? I wish I had brothers to get groceries.

Actually, I do have brothers. Before Ma, Pa had three sons from another woman. But I don't even know what they look like. I used to imagine them. I pictured them stopping bullies from bullying me. I pictured them giving me money when I wanted candy. I pictured them teaching me boy stuff Pa didn't.

Now I've stopped imagining them. They're not coming to Brooklyn for me, and they probably don't even know about me. Supposedly, they're grown and live in Philly or somewhere.

Pa probably doesn't even know what his sons look like either. Ma says Pa left them when they were like nine or ten and he hasn't seen them since. Whatevs.

So, I have to go get groceries. Not Ava. Not imaginary brothers. Me. And I *hate* it.

• • •

I look at Ma's shopping list. "Can I add chocolate powder?"

She sighs. "Bryan, we're just getting what we need."

"I need chocolate milk," I say. I look at the list again. "Okay, how about grapes? We need them."

"We have."

"They so shriveled," I joke, "they raisins now."

But Ma's in a serious mood. "Money is tight."

I want to say, *If money is tight and we have to buy food on credit, why you inviting Mike to dinner?*

But I just take the list and head for the elevator. When it shows up, there's a puddle of piss in it. Instead of someone cleaning it up, it looks like heads did what they usually do—keep trashing it. Junk-food wrappers and cigarette butts float on the puddle that stinks ammonia-strong.

I take the stairs.

• • •

Pa's friends hang out on the corner near the bodega.

His friend Pito lowers his sunglasses and waves when he sees me. Pito could pass for that basketball player Stephen Curry and always rocks skintight T-shirts that show off his abs, no matter how cold it gets outside.

A bunch of other familiar faces spot me and their faces flip from hard to hi, but not much else flips. Loud Spanish music thumps. Teens who rock the most dip gear sit on milk crates. Some of Pa's real old—viejo—friends sit at a table and play dominoes and beef about the last move made.

This is Pa and his homeboys' spot. I only come by when I'm on my way to the bodega or the arcade next door.

Ava says I don't like to hang here because I'm soft. That's why she calls me a momma's boy. I'm not a momma's boy, but I am like Ma since she got me used to being by myself, the way she keeps to herself.

"Focus on school," Ma always tells me. "There will be friends later. The wrong friends bring drama, and I don't want them rubbing off on you." Anyway, with all that advice, I wonder why she's letting Mike come over.

Nicholas, this black older man with dark skin and all-white hair like Magneto from the X-Men, puts his hand on my shoulder and nods at a crate. "Sit! Sit!"

"No thanks," I tell Nicholas real kind. "Ma and Pa want me back with the food."

Nicholas and Pa's friends circle me, smiling. Some are a bit bent with that same smell Pa has when he drinks. But the look in their eyes is the same: love. I *know* they have my back.

When me and Pa are here, he tells them, "Look out for my son," and they swear they'd body anyone who messes with me. Once, when Pa told Pito to look out for me, Pito lifted his fist, showed Pa his knuckles, and told him, "Joe, you kidding me? Someone messes with him and they get this." Pa lifted his fist too, and they winked, pumping fists like boxers before a boxing match.

I believe Pito and Nicholas and all of Pa's friends when they say they'll do whatevs for me. Out here, you need heads who got your back and it feels good that they got mine.

I go in the store.

• • •

"Bryan!" Hector smiles at me while humming along to a Marc Anthony song playing loud from behind the counter.

I hand him Ma's shopping list. He stops humming, reads it, and bites his lip. "Your father hasn't paid his last bill."

I look away, wishing I wasn't here.

Hector sighs and slides Ma's list on the counter back to me. "Go ahead. Tell him I'll add this to his old bill."

I grab it, then a handbasket, and walk in the Goya aisle.

I start getting stuff from shelves, and when I get to the bread, Hector's tiger-striped cat chills on top of a loaf.

I want to tell Hector, "Mercedes is smushing the bread."

I can't though. Hector might flip and say, "My cat can do what she wants. You don't even have money. Be happy I let you get food."

I walk up to Mercedes and the bread.

She hisses.

Ugh!

I try to grab a not-smushed bread, and Mercedes swats me *mad* fast!

Yo! Her eyes look like she says, *Get out my store with your broke butt.*

When I finally have everything, I go to the counter. Hector checks if the list matches what I got. I can't have nothing extra.

I stare back at the chocolate powder we can't afford to buy. Chocolate milk tastes *so good.*

Right then, this girl Melanie from my school comes in and watches as Hector bags my stuff and hands me a Post-it. "This is how much your father owes."

Dang! Why'd he have to mention us owing money? I nervous-smile at Melanie, and just like I thought, she eyes me all in my sauce and trying to know the flavor.

What's for her to figure out? I'm a broke joke.

Yo! I wish I could explode magician smoke in front of me and—*poof*—I'd be gone and not here, all embarrassed.

I nod at Hector. "Okay."

"Tell Joe I say hi."

Outside his store, I look above everyone's head—above all the laughs, the arguing, and the music.

I look toward Manhattan, and I wish things could be different.

I wish my family had more money.

I wish that girl didn't have to see me be broke.

I wish I had a brother for real.

I wish I wasn't in my feelings.

I wish I didn't care so much.

CHAPTER 3

Opening my apartment, I wonder if Pa is home and what mood he'll be in. He's not in the living room, so I head to his and Ma's bedroom. Their door is closed. Since I hear Ma in the kitchen, he must be in their room.

Pa's changed since he got out of jail this time. Instead of hanging in the streets with his homeboys, he's at home more—maybe trying to stay out of trouble. Anyways, him home more is different, but one thing isn't: He still spends zero time with me or Ava.

Sometimes when he comes out, I ask him to play dominoes but his answer is usually no. Why no? He brags to his corner friends that he's a pro because he played so much in jail. With us, though, it's like he doesn't want to be bothered, which is why I have to psych myself up to knock.

I know he doesn't like boys in our apartment around my sister so I'm thirsty to tell him Ma invited Mike to dinner.

Pa would want to know, I psych myself up some more. *He'll thank me.*

Knock-knock-knock.

"What?!"

"It's me," I say.

"Come in."

Pa sits up in his bed reading a newspaper, wearing his eye-glasses, in a tank top and his boxer shorts. He looks so peace-ful. No one seeing him this way would guess he's about that Thug Life in the streets.

"What?" He smacks his paper onto his lap.

"That boy Mike is coming here. Tonight. For dinner."

Pa's face flips to real warm as he moves his paper off his lap and gets up. "Good!" He slides his feet into his slippers, then walks by me and out the room.

Why does he look happy Mike'll be here for dinner?

I leave the room and find Pa in the kitchen talking to Ma. "What're you making?"

"I was just deciding," Ma tells him. "Mike is coming for dinner, okay?"

Pa bends over to peek in the fridge. "Bryan told me. We have Italian bread?"

Ma pulls one she hid on the top of the fridge. "Here."

Pa tells Ma. "I'll cook my jamón y queso tonight."

What?! I asked him the other day to make his ham-and-cheese special, and he said no. That's my favorite dish. *Now* he's cooking it? Why now all of a sudden?

What's the big deal about this Mike kid?

• • •

It's almost dinnertime, and Ava sets the table.

I poke my head in Ma's bedroom door as she folds laundry on her bed.

11

"Ma, you busy?"

She nods at my unfolded T-shirts on the corner of her bed. "Help fold. I shrunk your *Star Wars* shirt."

I bum-rush the bed and dig through my shirts mad fast because *that's* my favorite shirt. I find it and hold it up. *Whew!* "Why you say you shrank it? It didn't shrink."

Ma smirks. "I guess that's how I make you touch laundry."

"Nah. That's not funny," I tell her. But it worked. I start folding.

"Why's Mike coming for dinner?" I finally ask her.

"Well, Mike seems nice," she says, "and Pa and I thought he might make a good friend for you."

"Since when do you want me having friends? What happened to you saying no friends and I should focus on school?"

"I *know* Mike. He gets good grades. When his mother brought in her paperwork, she showed me his report card. And it's time to change from me telling you no friends because you're getting older and you need friends. Good friends."

"Okay. What about Pa?" I ask. "Why is he acting different because of Mike?"

"Pa's not."

I mumble, "Whatevs," and fold my *Batman* T-shirt.

● ● ●

Our apartment door slams.

I race into the living room, where Pa and Mike laugh about something. I'm too late for the joke.

Pa goes toward the kitchen and tells us, "Sit. Food's ready."

Ava sits *next* to Mike, and I sit next to Ma.

As we eat, Mike jokes, "You know what's better than melted cheese?" then nods at Pa, then Ava, who nod back at him. "Melted ham *and* . . . "

"*Cheese*," they finish his sentence.

Mike, Ava, and Pa laugh at themselves for saying the same thing at the same time like they're part of the same family together, and I'm not.

I try to join them and fake-chuckle.

Ava sneers at me like I farted something disgusting.

Yo! I'm *done*! I wish I could empty this Mike kid's plate in the garbage, grab his elbow, and shove him out my apartment so he falls flat on his joking face.

What's he trying to be funny for? It's *The Mike Show*, and I feel invisible and I only half listen while I lick melted cheese off my fingers.

But during one of his jokes, he turns to me and says, "Bryan, you know how this joke ends."

I have no idea what he's talking about, but I pay more attention because he's putting me on the spot.

Mike keeps telling his joke, then he ends with "So she tells him, 'This is an A and B conversation, so . . .' " He points his fork at me.

I *do* know how this joke ends! I say, "This is an A and B conversation, so C your way out."

Pa nods and winks at me. "That's a good one."

Then Mike says, "It was, like, he was all in the sauce and . . ." He points at me again.

I finish his sentence. "And he doesn't know the flavor."

Ma gives me a look like she's impressed. Even Ava looks at me like I'm not so disgusting anymore.

And Mike nods at me like I'm the man.

Pa stands and starts taking our plates to put in the sink. Ma stands to help.

Pa tells me, "Bryan, go get my dominoes. I want to see you and Mike play."

Dominoes? For real? I jet from the dinner table and rush back with them to the living room.

• • •

I pour dominoes on the folding table Pa set up for me and Mike. The sounds of the tiles clinking amps me up.

Pa stands over us. "Take seven," he tells us.

"Seven," me and Mike say at the same time, then we smirk a little at each other because we said *seven* at the same time.

I sit and hold my tiles the way Pa acts when he plays.

"Who has the double six?" Pa wants to know.

"Me." Mike clinks the domino on the table.

I clink a six-four.

We play a bit, and Pa stands on my side now.

He points at the five in my hand. "Count how many of those are on the table."

I do. Seven. Seven fives are on the table. One five is on Mike's end. I look at Pa, confused.

Pa winks. "There are eight in the whole pile."

I look back at my hand. That means I have the eighth five.

Pa points again at the five in my hand, then at the table. "Put that down and you lock the game and win."

I shift in my seat, too psyched to put my five down. I slap it on the table *hard*. The way I've seen Pa do. The way I think he'd want me to.

Pa rubs my head and goes toward the kitchen.

"Good game." Mike pours the dominoes in his hand onto the table. Then he spins one fast.

I watch it spin round and round, as Mike says, "I like doing this at the end of a game."

"You played before?" I ask.

"My moms taught me. She plays."

"You win a lot?"

Mike shrugs. "Usually, all my games."

He spins another domino. I look at him, wondering if he let me win.

After a few seconds, I realize I really don't care.

I just played dominoes.

Pa sorta played with me.

Pa just coached me.

Pa rubbed my head.

I watch Mike spin more dominoes and I wonder. Maybe Ma was right. Right when she said Mike is a nice kid and a cool friend to roll with. Because having him around maybe isn't so wack after all.

CHAPTER 4

"You like comics?" Mike asks after we finish our fourth dominoes game.

I do but I don't buy them on the regular since we don't have loot for them.

He rushes real quick to his backpack near the sofa, sits back across from me, and pulls out, like, seven comics. Each one is in its own see-through plastic bag. Like ziplocks for comics.

I lean in wanting to ask to see one, and before I can, Mike hands me half his stack.

"Open them," he says. "Just be careful. In a few years, each'll be worth mad much. That one right there is so boss it'll buy me one of those all-black Escalades Jay-Z be in. With tinted windows you can't see through."

I thumb at my room. "I have a comic. It's a'ight but it's busted because I . . ."

He asks, mad excited, "Can I go see?"

• • •

"This whole room is yours?" he asks as we walk in.

"Yeah."

16

Because it's my *only* comic, I hid it in a sneaker box under my bed. Now that I know Mike says comics will be worth bank one day, maybe I should put it up in a ziplock in my closet where I have my autographed poster from the Brooklyn Nets. I got that when my school went on a trip to the Barclays Center.

I find my comic, and Mike walks to the window with it for more light. He holds the comic mad close to his face like it's some precious treasure.

"Son, this is the first *Ultimate Spider-Man*! Where Miles Morales becomes the new Spider-Man!" He says this like he doesn't believe it.

I didn't know. I only bought it because the new Spider-Man in it is my age and looks like me. He's half black and half Puerto Rican. I'm full Rican but heads rarely guess right.

He asks, "You know how many of my comics is worth this?!"

I cock my head. "Word? A few is worth that one? I didn't—"

"Bryan, keep this, a'ight?" He interrupts me like he's OD serious. "*Never* trade it. I'm looking out for you. This is bank."

"It's wrinkled though." I point to wrinkly parts.

"Still."

"Still?" I ask.

"*STILL!*"

Mike stretches out on my bed mad fast and flicks through my Spider-Man comic.

I sit on the edge with his seven wavy, ziplocked comics: *Supermans*, *Batmans*, and a DC-Marvel crossover. I open and pull one out and check for his reaction but he's not taking his eyes off my comic.

He talks to me again but still doesn't take his eyes off what he reads. "Bust it!" He pops up on the bed, giddy. "This is where Miles comes out in the *Spider-Man* costume. He looks like you and your pops, Joe, you know that?" He holds the comic up to my head level next to my face and smiles. "You Spider-Man, Bryan? And I don't know it?"

What he just said has me feeling like I'm web-swinging high over Manhattan skyscrapers like Spider-Man.

"He looks like you too," I tell Mike. "Because me and you—"

"We could pass for brothers," he finishes.

I wasn't going to say that, but I like how that sounds. "Brothers."

Mike shuts my comic and scoots next to me.

He points to the page of the *Batman* comic I'm reading and tells me a secret fact about Robin. "Robin has no pops or moms, just like Batman." Mike keeps saying facts about Batman, the Joker, and more.

"How you know so much about comics? Where you learn all of this?"

He tells me he's been into comics for a while then tells me more facts about heroes and villains from comics that aren't even in this stack. Mike is a brainiac for real, for real. Like that genius kid David who used to be in my class and sounded too smart for my school. Then one day his parents transferred him out and I never saw him again. I believe Ma when she said Mike has good grades from when she saw his report card.

Mike keeps blowing my mind with more comic facts, then he suddenly sits straight.

"Out of these superheroes"—Mike holds a bunch of comics in both hands the way magicians hold up cards when they ask someone to pick one—"whose power you want?"

I point to Mike's *Batman* comic. Then to his *Black Panther* comic. "Them two. It says on *Batman*'s cover he's the world's smartest detective. Or I'd be Black Panther since he's as smart as Batman. They figure stuff out fast and know things ten steps ahead. Plus, they fight as good as anyone if they have to."

"Black Panther is smarter. Batman is one of the smartest people on Earth. Black Panther is one of the smartest people in the *whole Marvel universe*." Mike corrects me about that then holds up a comic. "But *this* is the man! Luke Cage. Nothing hurts him."

Luke Cage rocks a skintight T-shirt, has huge muscles everywhere, is black, and bald.

"Nothing?" I ask.

"Nothing. His skin can't break, he's strong like Superman, and he throws trucks. He'll run through this brick wall. Tobi at school has Netflix, and Luke Cage has a show."

"You have a phone? Show me."

Mike shakes his head. "Nah, I don't have one."

"Me neither," I say.

"But if I did," he says, grinning, "I'd show you Luke Cage's show and it's *sick*. In one episode, he stops a car racing at top speed just by stepping in front of it. I'm telling you: *Nothing* hurts him."

"Cool!"

When he gets ready to leave, Mike puts each comic back

into a ziplock, then stacks them in a pile. A piece of white copy paper sticks out a bit in between the comics.

"What's that?" I ask, pointing at it.

Mike slides it out and hands it to me.

Whoa! It's a blazing pencil drawing of Batman choke-holding the Joker while Superman floats above everyone and bullets bounce off his chest. I keep catching new cool parts of this drawing—details and shading making it hot enough to be in a comic. Mike's name is signed in the bottom left-hand corner.

"You drew this?" I ask, mad impressed.

He nods. "Yeah. It's not my best. I have better at home."

I can't believe dude is an artist. "Hold up!"

I go to the top of my drawer and bring down my sneaker box. "Check these out."

Mike flips through my drawings. Drawing after drawing, his nod goes from a little to a lot of nodding. "This is what's up! You draw too?"

"*Been*. Since third grade."

"Me too!"

Mike reaches his fist over to me and we fist-bump.

"I have to jet," Mike says. "But let's chill tomorrow. After school, maybe we could read comics and draw. At my place."

"That'd be cool."

We leave my room, and Mike says good-bye to everyone.

"Maybe you and Bryan should hang out again," Pa suggests. Ha!

Me and Mike nod at each other like we're in the same secret club together since we already privately spoke about that.

Mike asks Ma, "Can he come over my place tomorrow?"

She squints, thinking about it. "Will your mom be there?"

"Yeah."

"Okay, then," Ma says. I figure Ma is fine with it because she works late most weekdays, so now I'll have another safe place to be after school.

Me and Mike fist-bump each other again. "Tomorrow."

This is crazy. Just yesterday I wished things could be different. And now they are.

I was worried about Mike and now we cool.

Tomorrow is going to be lit.

CHAPTER 5

Mike's building is like mine. Outside, heads hang everywhere.

"Ayo!" one grown man jokes mad loud with Mike. "Who dis? Another brother of yours?"

A bunch of guys laugh like that's the funniest cut.

"Yeah," Mike says like it's true. "This is my brother Bryan."

Dudes nod and greet me. "Whattup, Mike's brother."

Some put fists and hands out. I fist-bump and dap back as me and Mike go in his building. I have to admit it feels good.

I head to Mike's elevator and he says, "Let's take the stairs."

His elevator must be like mine.

On the fourth floor, Mike uses his key to open his apartment door. It's quiet inside.

"Where's your moms?" I ask.

He shrugs like it's no big deal and says, "She'll probably be home soon."

What's up with homeboy? Did he lie to my mother? On one hand, I feel a bit uncomfortable. On the other hand, I figure it must be okay. I mean, Ma and Pa want me to hang with him.

In his bedroom, there's almost no room to walk, with three beds squeezed in. Now I get why he made a big deal about me having my own room. Now I get those times Ma told Ava and me we don't realize how good we have it.

Mike says, "I have three brothers."

My eyes pop. I have three brothers! But I don't even live with one, and he lives with all three.

"Yeah, one of them won't be here for a while. He went to live with his pops for I don't know how long. You want a *Superman*, a *Spider-Man*, or something better?"

"Whatevs. You said 'better.' Hook me up with better."

Mike grins and jokes in a high, whiny voice like that comedian Kevin Hart: "Oh, you not *ready*. '*He wasn't ready.*'"

He goes and kneels by his bed and slides out a sneaker box from under it.

Wooooow. He hides stuff in a sneaker box under his bed too.

He pulls two comics from it. "Bust *these*."

"*Daredevil!*" I read both covers' titles. "These covers are *lit!*"

Mike points at Daredevil, all built in his bloodred costume. "He moves like Spider-Man. He beats up guys left and right."

"C'mon, son," I interrupt Mike. "I *know* Daredevil. When he gets mad, he turns into a green giant who gets stronger as he gets madder."

Mike looks at me like I'm dumber than dumb.

I joke, "Gotti! Daredevil is blind! He can't see and uses a billy club to fight and swings above buildings like Spider-Man."

Mike laughs and exhales hard. "*Woo!* Good one. I thought for a sec you seriously confused Daredevil with the Hulk."

Mike takes one of the Daredevil comics and climbs on his bed. I stand there not knowing what to do.

"Sit there." Mike points. "That my brother's bed. The one who'll be ghost for a while."

I hop on it.

When I'm done with mine, we swap.

Then we get two new comics, finish, and swap again.

We swap so many times that at one point I stop reading and tell him, "Yo, my feet fell asleep."

"My butt *been* fell asleep," Mike says, laughing.

We both laugh as I punch feeling back into my legs.

Mike laughs, punching his butt.

We go back to reading, and soon it's dark out of his window and I realize I have to leave.

All that time, none of Mike's family ever came to his apartment.

When I get back home, Ma asks, "So how was it at Mike's?"

"Fine."

She doesn't ask if his mom was there, and I'm glad because I don't have to get into specifics.

Part of me figures Mike might've thought his mother was coming home and the next time she'll be there. But what if it is just me and him again the next time? Well, what's so bad about that? We did what Ma likes me doing: chilling, staying out of trouble, and we even read. Ma thinks reading is the best, so I guess it's all good.

CHAPTER 6

The next day I hang with Mike after school again in his apartment. I meet two of his brothers, Jim and Desmond. But they're jetting so we don't really speak.

His mom ends up being there for a little bit too. I meet her as I leave but she doesn't say much either. None of Mike's family stays long enough in each other's space for anyone to *talk*-talk.

The next week I'm glad when Mike says, "Let's head to your place." I'm happy because it's my place, and Ma said she'll be home early so she'll be around. That feels better to me. So just like that, we stop going to his apartment.

Once in my place, Mike points at a photo on the living-room shelf near the TV. It's of Pa and his friends from jail. They all rock prison uniforms. Nobody smiles. Mike grins and says, "They gangster."

I nod and tap his elbow. "Come on. Let's go over . . ."

He ignores me and leans toward the photo the way someone in a museum does when they want to study every little part of a painting. Mike's eyes trace Pa's face in the photo. "Your pops is the man."

"Yeah."

That makes me think of when I was little and Pa asked me, "Would you rather have people like you or be afraid of you?" Back then, I said I didn't know and Pa told me, "You want them afraid of you. If they're afraid, they'll respect you. Being respected is better than being liked."

"So how'd you get to know my pops?" I ask Mike.

"One day when your moms was helping us at the center, your pops was there. Your moms thought he should talk to me because my dad's not around."

I look at Mike. I wonder where his dad is.

"So from then on," he says, "if your pops saw me around the neighborhood, he looked out for me."

I knew that from the times Pa hit Mike off with change and advice.

It's funny how back before I knew Mike, it bugged me how Pa and Ma paid attention to him. But now that I know Mike is cool, I don't mind so much.

CHAPTER 7

Now that me and Mike are tight like brothers, we start sitting next to each other in our school cafeteria.

One day I notice him snarling like me. "Whattup?" I ask.

He nods across from us at this other sixth grader named James and whispers to me, "I want to pinch his lips shut. Why he chewing with his mouth all open? Disgusting."

I stare at Mike, not believing he just said that. James is why *I'm* snarling. It's gross when people chew with their mouths open.

Then that afternoon, we're in my elevator when this man in front of us tries to fart on the DL. The man *knows* what he just did is foul because he gets off on the second floor when he usually rides to five. The door closes and I tell Mike, "He deserves a neck for that."

"THIS is what *I'm* saying! Who farts in a closed elevator?! So nasty."

"We should've got off with him," I joke. "Smells like rotten eggs."

We bust out laughing at that.

The day after that, I realize another thing me and Mike can't stand. We pass by Pa's corner and Pa's back outside. He's in a huddle, kicking it with Pito and Hector from the corner store and there's that new guy, Alex. One day, he wasn't here. Then—*boom*—suddenly he was on the corner all comfortable, acting like he's been tight with everyone since forever. He moves people's plastic milk crates around without asking and sits where he likes. Pa turns to tell Hector something, and the look I see Alex give Pa gives me a bad feeling. Alex rocks a real fake smile like the comedian Steve Harvey has when he clowns someone. All teeth with sneaky, mean eyes.

Mike notices too. "Look at that snake," he says, pointing where my eyes are aimed. "That dude. How come his face is so ill as he eyes your pops?"

"That's Alex. Ma says he's no good."

Mike nods. "He looks sheisty. He best be careful with your pops."

"What do you mean?" I ask.

"I've seen your dad smack down a guy way more built than Alex. The guy was dissing old man after old man on your pops's corner. He must've thought your pops was soft because he's just chilling on his milk crate. Then he pointed at your pops, said something, stepped toward him, and—*yo!*—I didn't know your pops could move so fast. I almost didn't see it, but he jumped off that crate and smacked that young guy so fast!"

"Then what?"

"Then nothing," Mike says with a laugh. "The guy hit the ground—*boink!* Then your pops told everyone to get rid of that troublemaker before he really hurt him. They listened like bodyguards because your pops is boss and they dragged homeboy off the block."

Hearing Mike say this makes me feel all kinds of things. I eye my pops, sort of impressed. But I worry too—Pa's temper put him in jail. He's lucky he didn't get locked up over another fight. I look back at Pa and Alex, and I feel good knowing Pa can deal with him but I wish there was another way for Pa to dead drama without using his fists.

CHAPTER 8

"You saw that?" Mike asks me as he munches on potato chips he bought earlier.

A UFC Mixed Martial Arts fight is about to start on my TV. The fighters pace in opposite corners. Mike scoots to the edge of the bed and is mad hyped and taps his feet on the floor. "You saw him?"

I ask, "Who? And give me some of those chips."

Mike stands and points at the guy he means. "Him! *His* eyes."

Is he ignoring me asking him for chips on purpose? I look at the guy who Mike points at: the guy punching his gloves together over and over. I sit up because I've seen his kind of wild, bulging, googly eyes before on Pa.

"Who you think will win?" Mike licks his fingers, making those chips look extra good.

Both fighters got muscles from head to toe. Even though the one with the crazy eyes acts all intense and kray, the other has tats all over, even on his face. He looks scarier, so I pick him.

"You lose."

"You caught this fight before?" I ask.

"Nah," he says. "I didn't need to to know who wins. You ever hit someone or been in a fight?"

That makes me think of a long time ago. Waaaay before I met Mike, when I was in the third grade, my sister asked me to "make a fist." When I asked her why, she said, "Because you can't be soft out there. I don't want boys picking on you." But when I made a fist, she laughed. "You can't hold your thumb in your hand like that when you punch. You'll break your thumb. Forget it. I can't believe we family. You can't even throw a punch."

Right now, I stare at Mike and his bag of chips. "Nah," I finally say. "I never been in a fight. Why does it matter? Anyways, give me some chips."

"You *never* been in a fight?"

I shrug. "Who cares. I haven't. So what?" I stand and reach for his bag of chips.

"Nah." He moves his chips away. "Wooooow. You *never* been in a fight." He annoyingly repeats it like he's discovered some big treasure.

The fighters on TV stand face-to-face.

"Why you think my man won't win?"

"Like I said," Mike tells me, "look at their eyes. Look at the dude you picked. He looking left, right, and everywhere *except* at the dude he has to fight."

"But the dude I picked is more in shape and look at his tats all over. He looks scarier."

31

"I don't care *how* he looks. I don't care if he has tats on his lip. Look at his eyes: He's shook."

Mike has me curious. I want to see if his guess is right.

The ref says stuff, the fight starts, and soon me and Mike are so into the fight that Mike bobs and weaves where he stands and I throw short punches where I sit. I look at the corner of the screen that shows the time left in the round and—*boom*—my man gets snuffed, falls, and Mike's man sits on him and starts pounding on him. The ref tackles him off, and he's won and punches his fist against his chest, all braggy, and his eyes are cocky.

"Told you!" Mike punches his fist into his hand. "What I say?"

"Yeah. You got it."

I grab the remote to switch the channel. "You been in a fight?"

He laughs. "Too many. And if whoever I fight does what your man did and looks away when we start, I know I'ma beat him silly."

Maybe it's the way he says it. Maybe it's that he's been in a lot of fights. Mike makes me wonder.

I point at his potato chip bag. "Dude, share!"

He lifts the bag, taps the last chips left into his mouth, then talks all disgusting with his mouth full. "Not for you. I bought these for me. Plus, you picked the wrong fighter."

I look at him for mad long. His eyes look cocky like the fighter he picked.

For the first time since we started chilling, I feel different about Mike. I feel like I don't know the whole him.

When he showed up at Ma's desk, I felt this way, then got to know him and the feeling went away. But it's back. I don't know if I should trust my original bad vibe about him, or just move ahead and trust him?

CHAPTER 9

On Friday, Ma finishes stuff at her desk at work. Her work-day was over ten minutes ago. I sit in my pretend-office doing nothing really. Just waiting for Ma while smacking a handball from hand to hand as long as I can without letting it fall. Doing this helps make my hand-eye coordination better for handball games.

"Are you ready?" Ma interrupts me.

"Yeah," I say, snatching the ball midair and grabbing my book bag.

Ma leads me in the opposite direction we usually go, away from the projects, and holds my hand. Only a few boys out here hold their moms' hands. Most act too cool to even walk close to their moms. I don't sweat Ma holding my hand because she's my heart and we're tight and I don't hide it.

I thumb behind us in the direction of our block. "Where we going?"

Ma winks. "I have a surprise."

I have a feeling I know where she taking me. That cuchifrito spot that makes slamming fried Spanish food. The cooks there bag the food in brown paper bags, and the grease stains expand from pencil-point dots to stains the size of my fist! The food makes my hands, lips, and cheeks mad oily, but I don't care. It's all sooo good: alcapurrias with this crunchy hard outside but a chopped meat center; papas rellenas with a fried potato shell that makes me feel like I'm eating a baseball-shaped French fry; and chicharrones with salty, crunchy chicken so good that KFC can't even mess with it.

I smile. "Good thing I'm hungry!"

She pinches my cheek. "So you think you know where we are going, huh? You're psychic now?"

I nod.

Two blocks from La Estrella—the cuchifrito spot—Ma turns right instead of left to the restaurant. She grins. "Are you still psychic?"

Right as we get to the bus stop, the bus that rides out of our projects toward downtown Brooklyn pulls up.

"Hurry." Ma tugs at my hand. "That's us."

After we climb on, I ask, "Where are we going?"

"I'll give you a hint"—she lifts three of her fingers—"but you have to name three of your favorite superheroes."

I speak so fast that it sounds like I say one word. And I'm so loud that grown people on the bus turn their heads and smile at me. "Batman, Black Panther, and Flash!"

"Okay." She smiles. "So that's the hint."

I speak fast and louder than I did before, and the same grown people turn and smile at me. "You're taking me to the movies!"

35

Ma nods.

I scoot close to her and hug her harder than hard.

• • •

After the movie, Ma adds extra sweetness to our chilling. She takes the refillable tub of popcorn before we leave the theater and asks me, "Want to refill it?"

Ma hasn't done this in a while with just me. I remember the last time was the day after there was a fire in an apartment on my block. Fire trucks with loud sirens felt like they were on our street forever. The sound was too much for me. So the next day, Ma brought me to this movie theater, and it was so quiet before the movie started and so quiet after. Once the movie ended, I didn't want to leave. I wanted to stay in that quiet, live in that theater with Ma. So I asked her, "Can we sit here for just a little?" And we did. We talked as everyone left until we were the only ones left sitting there. The lights flicked on and we talked some more. Then Ma asked, "How do you feel right now?"

"Peaceful."

"Do you like it?"

"Yes. I like it quiet."

Ma soft-pinched my chin. "Me too."

The people who sweep the theater came in. When they got to our row, I jumped up to help them, grabbing empty soda cups and candy wrappers to run to them. "Here you go, sir."

Back then, one worker told me, "No. You don't have to help," then told Ma, "Your son's a good kid." The other worker watching agreed. "He's real respectful."

Back then, right before we left that movie's building, Ma

36

was about to throw out the tub, and I asked her, "Can we refill it? Go somewhere? Keep talking?" And we did. Ma took me to Brooklyn Heights. When we stepped on the long boardwalk of cement that Ma called the Promenade, my jaw dropped. I said, "We see all of Manhattan!"

"Bryan, that's only one tip of Manhattan."

Right now, Ma's telling me she wants to refill the tub of popcorn makes me think she might be taking me there. Then she reads my mind. "Want to go to the Promenade?"

• • •

At the Promenade, we sit on a bench and keep reaching in the tub and eating fistfuls.

The view is as whoa as I remember, as day turns to night and the sky becomes a painting of rainbow colors over Manhattan's twinkling skyscrapers.

It's so peaceful and I get so comfortable that I sit crisscross-applesauce and face Ma to keep talking. Back in the projects, I wouldn't sit on a bench this way. I'd get called soft for sitting and being all expressive. But Ma doesn't judge me. With her, I can sit any way and say anything—even the smallest, silliest stuff—and I like that.

Ma leans forward and asks me questions about the movie like she really wants to know my answers. Like my answers are important. And I start feeling important. Ma gets me all the way open as I speak and explain why I wish I could move like Flash but want Black Panther's and Batman's smarts, even though the Flash is supposed to think at the speed of light and more.

The whole time we eat popcorn and talk, something is sweeter than the treats: this feeling of chillness, of no drama, of peace. It's a peace I wish I could bring back to my projects and feel all the time.

CHAPTER 10

It's almost nine at night and my foot hurts because I'm lying in my bed with no shoes on and kicking the wall.

That's my way of telling Ma and Pa to stop arguing. Sometimes my kicking the wall hard makes them get quieter. Sometimes Ma comes in, sits on my bed, and helps me control my temper. "Breathe," she'll repeat, "breathe."

Right now, she does neither.

Pa barks at Ma, "Go ahead! Call my probation officer! You want me back in jail! Because when I'm out all you do is tell me what's wrong with me. I'm the problem! So, get rid of me! Get rid of the problem!"

I start feeling nervous when he yells like this. It's been a while because Pa was acting quieter when he first got out of jail. But now, he's acting like his old self. He's back to yelling, and when his voice gets to this level, he's about to explode.

I'm also nervous at the thought that Ma might call his PO.

I stop kicking and my insides hurt more than my foot.

Ma screams back, "Joe, you fight in the streets! Then you come home and fight! All you want to do is fight, fight, fight!"

"I didn't even want to fight!" he claps back. "I just was going in the kitchen and you didn't have to say, 'Be careful,' that way. Like I'm an idiot!"

"I didn't say it like that. You exploded for no reason."

"What! Now I'm deaf? I heard you wrong? You know what? My friend Alex is right. You think you're better than me."

"Who's Alex to tell you anything? Why're you letting that loser poison your head? He's jealous of you. And why do you listen to all those guys so much? All they do is get you in trouble!"

"I'm leaving!"

"Then leave!"

The door slams and then it gets quiet. Too quiet.

I hear my sister's music turn on. She was listening to them fight too.

Then I hear music turn on downstairs in 3A in Ms. Bernadine's apartment. She's so nosy and was listening to Ma and Pa fight too.

The whole building probably heard everything.

I listen to Ava's happy music and think there is nothing happy about our apartment right now.

● ● ●

"*You seen Pa?*" I whisper to Ava.

It's seven something in the morning, and Ava is still in bed buried under her covers. Only her nose and mouth peek out.

"*No!*" she hisses real salty, and rolls away from me.

She hates waking up early for school.

I stand there, OD upset about Pa. And I'm OD upset too that

she doesn't care. I shake her real soft, whispering again, "*Ava. Pa didn't come home last night. He always came home before.*"

Ava barks all loud, "Leave me alone and let me sleep!"

She buries herself so only her nose and mouth peek out again.

I'm so mad Pa isn't home. I'm so mad Ava won't help me know why. Something in me just pops!

I yank the covers right off her and run!

"MMMPH!" She swings and punches and kicks the air.

I'm already racing out her room toward the bathroom to lock myself in.

• • •

"Don't think I forgot you snatched the covers off me," Ava tells me as she pours herself cereal.

I look at her. Something about her face says she isn't really mad at me. She's tight about Pa and Ma's argument too.

Then Ma comes in the kitchen and rubs my head and strokes Ava's cheek.

She asks if we want her to make us breakfast.

"No," we both say.

Maybe we both say no because she looks so sad.

I wolf cereal down fast because I want to jet before Ava can get me back for pulling her covers.

I dump the bowl and spoon in the sink and rush and hug Ma. "I love you."

Right as I get to the door, I hear, "Bryan."

Ugh! It sounds like Ava's following me out to get even after all.

But in the hall, Ava's face flips. "That was crazy with Pa and Ma last night."

I know it takes a lot for her to say this because she usually doesn't talk about Pa and Ma fighting.

"Sometimes"—Ava looks back at our apartment door—"I wish Pa would just chill, you know?"

"Where you think he went?"

"He's fine. He'll just come home later like nothing happened."

"I hope so," I say.

"Yeah, anyways. You good?"

I nod. "You?"

She smiles, not a happy one but one that says she'll be all right. "Yeah. Be good in school."

• • •

There are two ways to my school.

I go the way to pass Pa's corner, and Ava was right. Pa's fine and he's right there with Pito and Nicholas. I'm happy not to see Alex.

Pa looks across the street at me, and we lock eyes for a couple of secs. It feels like forever. It feels like Pa's face shows ten different feelings at once.

He's probably embarrassed to be out here grungy in the same clothes. He's proud and likes to shower, shave, and wear fresh clothes every day. Right now, he's wearing the clothes he wore yesterday, and his face is all stubbly.

I cross the street and want to hug him. But we just stand a couple of feet apart and nod.

"You ate?" Pa asks.

"Yeah," I tell him.

I want to ask him if he ate.

I want to ask him where he slept last night.

But I don't.

Pa reaches in his pocket, pulls out some dollars, and hands it to me.

Since forever, Pa's used money as a way to apologize or make me feel like he cares. That's how come he's handing me it now.

"Go. Go to school. You need something, I'm here."

I want to say, *I don't need "something." I need you.*

But I leave.

Half a block away, I look back at him.

He still looks at me.

His face: It's like he wants to say a lot to me.

I want to say a lot to him.

He brushes his hand in the air like I should go. So I do.

CHAPTER 11

"Superman versus the Hulk," Mike says when I bump into him at the water fountain outside our school library.

"Superman," I say as we walk into the stairwell and head downstairs. "His heat vision will burn two holes through Hulk's skull. Fry his brain into smoke. Hulk or Colossus?"

"Hulk! He'll twist Colossus into a metal pretzel. Then fling him into outer space past the moon. Daredevil or Batman: no weapons, just hand-to-hand combat?"

"Daredevil," I say. "He has super-hearing, better than a bat's. He'd hear Batman's fist or kick way before they'd reach Daredevil's body. He'd hit Batman three, four times before Batman could connect."

We get to the second floor, where both our classes are, but Mike taps me to keep following him. When we get to the first floor, we keep walking and I'm about to ask where he's going when—all of a sudden—Mike pushes open an exit door and we see outside to the teachers' parking lot.

Mike steps outside but still holds the door open.

I wonder why the alarms don't go off and nothing happens.

"We could leave," Mike says. "Anytime."

"Yeah, but—"

"We won't get caught," Mike interrupts. "I've done it before. A lot in my old school. We could go the comic store in Carroll Gardens. They let you read as many comics as you want and you don't have to pay for them. There's a comic store in Manhattan we could hit that lets you do that too."

"Yeah, but—"

"I'm just showing you," Mike says and shuts the door. He gives me a disappointed look. "C'mon. Let's go to class."

• • •

A little after dismissal, I meet Mike outside of school so we can hit the arcade with the money from Pa.

As we get near Pa's corner, I see him kicking it with Alex, Pito, and Nicholas. Pa turns to tell Nicholas something, and I get a bad feeling when I see Alex rock that fake smile again.

Mike catches Alex's fakeness too. "Eww," he says. "There goes that fake snake with your pops again."

"Alex." I suck my teeth. "Ma was saying he's a real loser."

"She right."

Me and Mike dip into the arcade next to Hector's corner store.

And just like that . . . No conversation about earlier. No conversation about anything really. Except us asking questions like:

"What's your highest score you ever had?"
"You ever got to the board when you eat the big energy
pellets but the ghosts don't turn blue?"

"You like slow or fast Ms. Pac-Man better?"

*"Why didn't you eat the banana? It's like five thousand
    points."*

I'm slaying Mike by like two thousand and something points. He's down to his last life, and I still have four lives.

Then, through the side of my eye, I see Mike staring at me in a way I've never seen him stare at me before. Like Alex with that Steve Harvey fake smile we just saw him give Pa.

Maybe because *Ms. Pac-Man* has me feeling amped and I'm trying hard not to get eaten, my words come out mad forceful. "Dude, why you looking at me that way?"

Mike's smile changes. "Nah, not you. I'm staring at the screen."

I can't read his face to tell if he's lying because my eyes are on the screen.

I go back to focusing extra hard on my game because that ghost Pinky almost caught me.

"I have to be out," Mike says. "My moms expects me home."

He dips.

I stay.

While I play, Big Will from the sixth-grade class next to mine walks in. Heads joke that he has more facial hair and muscles than any sixth grader, ever. He also has better grades than most sixth graders and is on the honor roll. He geeks all the way out, but nobody messes with him the way they clown most nerdy boys in my projects.

He stands behind me and stares over my shoulder at my screen as I play.

"Dang!" he says when I almost die but shake off three ghosts.

"Yo!" He's shocked when I U-turn faster than fast to eat all the ghosts.

"Bryan," he gasps when I make it to the level where ghosts don't turn blue and can't be eaten. "I never knew they had *this* level."

I keep trying to hide my grin, but Big Will's props have me feeling wavy.

The next thing I notice is his face as he sees my points equal the high score, then pass it. He's not even hiding his smile.

Real quick, I turn my head because I want to get a full view of his expression. He's impressed. I feel like the man. Quicker than quick, I turn and look back at the screen so I don't mess up.

Soon, I'm five hundred points higher than the new score.

"WHOA!" I hear Big Will say.

I don't know whether it's his props or whether I'm just extra good today, but I end up posting the highest high score I've ever seen on this *Ms. Pac-Man* screen.

When my game is over, I turn to Big Will, and he gives me this pound and we shake. His hand is dumb strong like Pa's grown friends who forget I'm a kid and shake my hand OD hard.

I slip two quarters in to play again.

As I dodge ghosts, I start feeling that rush again.

I jam my joystick hard to the right and race *Ms. Pac-Man*

into a side exit that teleports me onto the left side of the screen away from the blue ghost who almost just got me.

Big Will says, "BAM! You like Neo dodging bullets in *The Matrix*!"

I'm so in the zone I don't hear Pa walk in and stand behind me and Big Will.

"I'm going home," Pa says.

Pa doesn't usually come in here for me. I think he wants me to go home with him so Ma'll let him in because she's probably still mad at him about their fight. I just want him home. I U-turn *Ms. Pac-Man* so she runs into a ghost and gets eaten.

I hate killing my men on purpose when I play, especially now when I've earned an extra life and have four instead of the three I started with. But Pa is going home.

I'm about to kill the rest of my men when Big Will asks, "Why you deading them for?"

Then it hits me. He might want to play.

"Will," I say, without taking my eyes off the screen, "grab this joystick."

And bust it: He does, and as I back away, I see his whole face change. He's lit. And I feel a little boss being able give away a game.

Me and Pa leave, and as we're at the door, Big Will calls to me without taking his eyes off his screen: "Bryan! Thanks for the hookup!"

I yell back, "No doubt," feeling even more boss.

CHAPTER 12

Pa never talks when we walk outside together. We could walk as far from our projects as twenty-three blocks away to Downtown Brooklyn and the only time he'd open his mouth is to kick it with strangers or heads he knows.

With us not talking, my mind goes back to Mike's fake smile in the arcade. Was he really just thinking about something else, like he said, which would explain his face? Whatever the truth is, I figure I'll watch Mike's expressions more.

When we walk into the apartment, Ma's reading a piece of Ava's homework to her. She stops and looks up at Pa.

He looks at Ma, then disappears into their bedroom.

I stand there for a minute and wait for her to ask me something about where I found him.

Finally, she just asks, "How was your day at school?"

"I . . ." I don't know what to say.

"You were at the arcade," Ma says.

"How'd you . . . ?"

Ava and Ma chuckle like they both see mud smeared on my face.

49

"What?" I wipe my cheek. "What?!"

"Your eyes," Ma says. "They always have this 'look' after you play."

"BOING!" Ava motions like I have bulging, googly eyes. "All intense, like you kray."

Ma nudges Ava. "Don't say that about him."

Ava ignores her and says, "*Eww! Don't stare at me like that, Bryan. Now you look extra kray.*"

Ma taps the book on Ava's lap they were just reading. "Let's finish."

Ma starts reading a science problem out loud.

I don't appreciate Ava saying I look crazy so I pass real close to her on the couch so I can dis her on the DL before I go into the bathroom to wash my hands for dinner.

But as soon as I get close enough to Ava, she mouths at me on the DL first, *You look crazy like Pa.*

I want to ask her, "What do you mean?" but I know what she means. That I look hyped, wild, and out of control. Looking like that is the last thing I want. But I know she's right because I feel that way. And suddenly I hate it—I hate feeling so hyped and almost out of control.

I hate feeling like Pa can get.

• • •

Nothing happens the rest of the night.

We have dinner as a family: me, Ma, Pa, and Ava.

Ma and Pa don't fight. They don't talk to each other, but that's cool since they're not fighting. They just hand each other stuff and get out of each other's way.

Nothing happening was the best.

So, when Mike yells my name from outside my window, asking to come up, I stick my head out and lie, "Can't. My moms wants me to do chores."

I sit back down on my bed, feeling real happy. There's a peacefulness to my apartment that's like the afternoons at Ma's job when no phones ring and all I can hear from my pretend-office are the sounds of Ma's coworkers' pencils scratchy-scribbling on paper or fingers tapping on computer keyboards. Everything is chill and there's not an ounce of drama. I love it. I look out my window and realize something. I helped make this moment chill, by what I chose. I think about that over and over, and I like it.

CHAPTER 13

I hear Mike on my way to school before I see him.

"Bryan! Hold up." He jogs to me. "You finish all your chores last night?"

For a second, I don't remember what he's talking about. "Ye ... yeah."

"Want?" He holds out his Sour Patch bag.

Finally! Dude's sharing instead of taking.

I dig in his bag and count with my fingers how many to take.

"Take mad much," he says. "I have another bag."

Ma doesn't like me having candy in the morning, but she's not here. Oh well! I pop a handful in my mouth and an eye winks shut. "Dang! Sour!"

He smiles. "But good though."

We fist-bump a "no doubt." As I lick sugar off my fingers, these questions come to me. Mike's fake smile as I played *Ms. Pac-Man*: Is dude real or fake? True or a liar? Then one question shoots out without me meaning to ask it. "Yesterday, you meant it about cutting school?"

He looks real hard at me. Then he checks so no one else can

hear. "If you had a choice, which would you choose? Stay in a boring class or be out? I mean, if you knew you could be ghost and not get in trouble?"

There are a couple of classes that are mad boring—Mr. Peters and Mrs. Donalds never teach. They hand out worksheets and make us work silently the whole period. I'd skip their classes if I, for sure, for sure, wouldn't be in trouble.

"How won't you get in trouble?" I ask. "Teachers take attendance in *every* class. Morning teachers would mark us present, then teachers later would mark us absent."

"You too worried about getting caught?" he says. "You not thinking."

"What?"

He unzips his book bag and shows me two pieces of paper. "Which is my moms's handwriting?"

I tap his left hand's note. "Fake."

"Wrong."

"Okay. So?"

"So, if you can't tell, neither can teachers. I write notes to my teachers in my moms's handwriting saying I won't be in school. And guess what?"

"What?"

"They excuse me. Then I hit the comic stores. Who writes notes to your teacher?"

"My moms."

Mike soft-punches my arm. "Then learn her handwriting. Write one of these, your teachers believe it, you miss a day, and we hit a spot I told you about."

I read Mike's face for a few seconds. Is he for real?

"Cutting school is wrong." As I say it, I realize I sound like my moms.

Mike just stares me.

I don't know what to think about him anymore. He flips-flops, showing the world one side of him, then he'll show another like this. "But what about your grades? My moms said you get good ones. How you do that if you cut classes?"

He wrinkles his face like I haven't been paying attention. "My grades don't drop because I get excused and make up the work. I do extra good in school, so people don't ever think I do stuff like this. See, it's easy."

All of a sudden, James from the other sixth-grade class runs up and tries sticking his hand in Mike's Sour Patches bag without asking. It's the same James who ate with his mouth all open in the cafeteria and disgusted me and Mike.

Mike smacks James's neck, hard and mad obvious, and I notice a bunch of kids watching, including Melanie, the girl from my grade who saw me in Hector's bodega getting food on loan.

"That's a neck, bruh," Mike says to James. "And the word you forgot is *please*."

James holds his hand out. "Please."

Instead of pouring some in James's hand, Mike pours the rest of the bag in his own mouth. There's mad much to share but he doesn't.

James's eyes pop wide, shocked by Mike's playing him.

Mike munches while rapping this girl-song from back in the day to James, but in a hard way so it sounds gangster. "My name is no, my sign is no. Bruh, you need to let it go." He flicks the empty Sour Patch bag at James, who catches it all stupid.

James looks tiiiiight, does nothing for a second, then flicks it back at Mike. "Dummy, I ain't your trash man."

I try not to laugh at James getting clowned, partly because it's foul, but mostly because Melanie is staring at Mike with a low-key stank face and at me like I'm an idiot for being with him.

Ugh. I walk away and ahead toward school.

• • •

Before dinner Ma sends me to the store and I pass guys who usually chill in front of Mike's building. One says, "Whattup," and another asks, "Where your brother?"

I used to think it was so cool when everyone thought Mike was my brother. And that having one would make life easier. But now I'm not sure.

I know having a sibling is hard sometimes—me and Ava fight too. Still, I know she always has my back. With Mike, I never know for sure.

CHAPTER 14

Monday after school me and Mike head back into our projects bragging about slaying dudes at the handball court. He bet this kid Charles Charles's bag of candy that we'd rock him and his friend in a doubles game. We did. Then rocked two more kids. Then another team.

"Son," Mike says, "that was sick when Charles ran left but you hit the ball right! And you had him looking like this . . . " He crosses his eyes and says, "Duhhh!"

I laugh. "Yeah, and your aces, man. Sick! Luis was *tight* every time you'd serve the ball too fast for him to hit, then you'd say—"

"*ACE!!!*" we both yell. "IN YOUR *FACE!*"

I imitate how Luis swung and missed the ball. Then I fall to exaggerate how off-balance he looked.

Mike busts out laughing.

After we leave the stadium's courts, me and him walk the long way around the edge of our projects to avoid Crazy Corner. Our projects has some wild guys to avoid and some of the wildest be on Crazy Corner. It's in the middle of our projects and even though there is a church and a supermarket, the block is run by a group of No Joke guys who all dress alike and travel in a crew. You mess with one, you mess with them all.

At the end of the block Mike taps me. "Want to do something fun?"

I'm still amped from handball and from joking, so I say, "Yeah."

He turns and walks toward a random building.

"You know someone in here?" I ask.

"Yeah, you?"

"Nah."

We go in and into the elevator. He presses five.

"Who we visiting?" I ask.

He starts banging this sick hip-hop beat on the metal walls of the elevator with his pen and fist. He beatboxes to the beat with his eyes closed like he's in a zone and can't hear me.

Out of the elevator, we walk up to the sixth floor. "You been on the roof?" he asks.

I start remembering in my head when I first learned our buildings had roofs. "Yeah," I say, "I—"

"Cool. Then come." He races up two steps at a time, and I follow.

Busting onto the roof, gravel crunches under my feet, and the view is *whoa!*

I see past our projects to Prospect Park in Park Slope. Prospect's treetops look like broccoli. I start doing a one-eighty turn and catch the Statue of Liberty wave at us. "We can see the piers from here."

"And Staten Island." Mike points left. Then right. "And New Jersey. And Manhattan."

I pinch the Empire State Building between my fingers. I get that feeling again. Like I'm bigger. Like I'm way above everything. I joke, "I'm lifting the Empire State Building."

Mike pinches the air too.

"What you lifting?" I ask.

"Our school." He sucks his teeth. "Get outta here!" He pretends to throw our school away. "Pitch that bum-butt school right in the river."

I chuckle under my breath.

Mike peeks over the wall. "You should look down," he tells me. "Downstairs, people look like ants. You know Rick in eighth grade? The one taller than everybody? He's down there and looks like a roach."

Rick's an annoying guy who always pats kids on the head as if he's their parent. He's never done that to me and he better not, or I might bite his ankles off or something.

I move to where Mike is. But standing *on* the roof is one thing. Standing *at* the edge is another. I don't want to fall seven flights and *SPLAT*. I stop walking because my heart beats so hard and fast that I feel it in my throat.

"You scared?" he asks.

"Nah." I pause. "I'm . . ."

"My first time on the edge I was scared." He faces me and leans on the wall, all relaxed, like it's nothing to him to be at the edge. "I thought I was gonna have a heart attack. But it goes away. Look! Watch this!"

He pulls himself up and sits on it. His feet dangle in the air.

"C'mon. You soft?" he says. "I can hold your hand like a baby if you want."

He's trying to punk me. I hate when people do that.

Breathe. Breathe. Don't let him punk you.

I lift my foot from where I'm planted and I swear it's like I'm lifting my foot out of cement. All my fear weighs my foot down. But I do it! I drag one foot forward.

Mike starts laughing at me.

Seeing him smirk like I'm a chicken makes me lift my other foot. I slowly walk to him like I'm some mummy. Then I'm right next to him . . . at the wall.

"Now, look over," he dares me.

It takes my whole everything to look over the edge. And . . . Mike is right. Rick looks like a roach—a swagged-out roach because he always rocks Jordans and dip gear. He is right about heads down there too. They dots and scurry like ants.

I'm about to tell him that the view is crazy cool, but before I can open my mouth, he pitches a pebble off the roof fast, then ducks out of sight.

What did he just do?!

I hear a car screech and I stare over the ledge.

"*Duck, stupid!*" Mike hisses at me. "You *want* someone from the street to look up and bust us?"

I duck, staring real angry at him. He rolls on the roof and starts laughing, like his throwing that rock was the funniest thing in the world.

I want to punch him, kick him, for so many reasons, including calling me stupid. That's disrespect.

But mostly I wonder . . .

What happened with that car that he just hit?

Did someone get hurt?

Do we know the person?

What is up with Mike?

It's like all these feelings and thoughts are the fastest birds in my head and I can't grab one.

Mike gets up and brushes gravel off him. "Let's be out before someone realizes we did this."

I want to yell, *WE?! We* didn't do this. *YOU* did this.

But he's already sprinted across the roof. I follow him to a faraway door that we didn't use before.

He dips in. "Shhh. Always come off the roof quiet. Heads might be leaving their apartment to throw trash out or something."

We creep down the steps like ninjas, making no sounds.

I go to press the elevator and Mike stops me. "You dumb? We have to take the steps. If someone saw us and traps us in the elevator, it's a wrap."

But by the time we reach the fourth floor, we don't sneak anymore. We hop down the flights, three, four steps at a time.

Before we come out of the stairwell at the first floor, he puts his hand on my chest. "Be cool. Walk out like we just came from visiting someone. Matter of fact, let's make it up right now. We came from Four-A."

"Four-A," I repeat.

"Visiting who?"

I'm so stuck on his calling me stupid and dumb and afraid we'll get caught, I don't know if I can play it cool.

Mike squints at me. "Wake up, bruh. Who we visited?"

"Oh! Oh, um, Tim . . . No, Cameron. Cam."

He nods. "Cam then. We go to school with him, right. That's the story."

"Bet."

He nods, we take deep breaths, then walk outside.

Once on my block, we say peace and split up.

After what just happened, I had enough of Mike to last me a week. I don't need to see *any more* of him today.

• • •

Everything that happened with Mike stays on my brain. It stays on my brain as I do my homework. It stays on my brain as I eat dinner. It stays on my brain as everyone goes to separate rooms to do their own things before bedtime.

He has me all types of confused.

I walk into the living room to find Ma but wanting to ask her if she really, *really* thinks Mike is someone I should rock with.

Ma's on the couch, looking tired. She looks up from her crossword puzzle and smiles. "So, how was your buddy Mike? Did you have fun today?"

She looks so happy about our friendship, and I think she doesn't need anything more to stress about.

"Yeah, we hung. He's fine."

Ma nods, still smiling.

"I'm going back in my room." I stuff my hands in my flannel pj's pockets.

"Did you want to talk about something?"

"Nah."

I go stand in the doorway to Pa's bedroom, imagining he's here. I imagine we could talk. But his bed is empty. He's out hanging. Anyway, that wouldn't happen—him giving me time to talk about stuff.

I leave and find Ava in the bathroom, brushing her teeth.

She knows I'm in the bathroom doorway but she doesn't look at me. "What, Big Head?"

"You think Mike is cool peeps?" I ask.

She gurgles and spits. "You probably questioning him *because* you soft."

There that word goes again: *soft.*

She turns and stabs her toothbrush in my direction. "So, what? You can't handle hanging with Mike?"

I grind my teeth. I stiffen my lip. I want to tell her everything he did. But she'll probably just think he's cooler. She'll probably think I'm soft for not seeing that he was just having fun. Guys' fun.

A part of me wonders if she's right.

CHAPTER 15

"Jessie! Jessie!" Someone bangs real loud on our apartment door, shouting Ma's name.

It's 2:12 in the morning.

Ma is already walking into the living room, tying her robe shut.

Me and Ava join her, and Ma hugs us both close.

"Who's knocking?" Ma says.

"Jessie! It's Mina!" the voice screams through our door. "They arrested Joe!"

I look at Ava. Ava buries her face in Ma's robe, trying not to show her feelings.

Ma opens the door to Mina. Ever since Ma helped Mina and her kids get out of a shelter and get housing here, Mina has done whatever she could for Ma. Mostly that means Mina hooks Ma up with gossip about people around here. Right now, the gossip is about my dad.

Mina speaks so fast it's kind of hard to follow. "Joe was hanging with Alex on the corner, you know. And I saw him walk away. Maybe coming home to you. So he was half a block away when Alex yelled at someone in a car about how he'll smack the crap out of him. All the doors on the car flung open, and these guys jumped out. And they started beating Alex. Joe U-turned to help Alex out. Then those guys started to run toward Joe. And you know Joe's not soft, so I heard he pulled out a knife. And then the cops got there, like"—Mina snaps her fingers—"*this* fast. I heard they yoked up Joe, but I also heard that as soon as they rolled up, he got rid of his knife."

Ma's hand flies to her jaw. She tries holding herself together.

"Don't worry, Jessie," Mina tells Ma. "They didn't find no weapon on Joe and since he doesn't have any priors, he should get out in a coupla days if you go to the precinct."

All of a sudden, there's this silence in our apartment. A loud silence. A silence that hurts.

Because I know and Ava knows and Ma knows the truth. Pa has priors that Mina doesn't know about. Mina thought Pa was out of jail, period. He's not. He's on probation.

This arrest means he's heading back.

• • •

After Mina leaves, Ma locks the bottom and top locks. Ava comes over and wraps an arm around me like everything will be okay. Then Ma comes over and hugs us both close.

Later, I don't go to bed.

Not even after Ma clicks Ava's door shut and leaves her room.

Nah, I'm not sleeping because Ma's not.

I hear Ma's chanclas slap the floor as she paces back and forth. *Slap-slap-slap.*

It's dumb early. They call it three "in the morning" but this type of morning looks like night. Lonely night. Bottle and can collectors aren't even out digging through trash.

Slap-slap-slap.

Ma probably thinks her slippers are quiet, but, right now, each slap has surround sound, especially because our block is OD dead, and we're all living with knowing Pa just got locked up.

I go rest my chin in my crossed forearms on my window ledge and I stare out my window into the night.

I turn and the *Luke Cage* comic that Mike loaned me is on my chair.

Luke rocks a skintight tank top. Bullet smoke steams off his chest, shoulder, and arm muscles. The bullets' shells are at his feet.

He is unbreakable. I wish I was him.

Now I wonder what Pa looks like in his jail cell, and I feel a tear streak out my eye. Then my other eye.

It's like earlier I had a dam in me, but now it's cracked and I'm leaking.

I lie on my bed on my side and grab a fistful of blanket and squeeze and cry. I can't breathe. I grip the blanket harder, crying harder.

I sit up and tell myself, "Breathe, *breathe.*" And I think, *Mike is smart. If I could choose again, I'd be Luke Cage.*

CHAPTER 16

The morning after Pa got arrested, I go to school more tired than I've ever been.

In every class, I'm dog-tired.

I stroke my chin; my face feels numb. I look at my fingers lying there all lifeless on the desk, and they don't even feel like they belong to me.

In gym, heads run and shout this and that way but it's all dead to me.

Lunchtime is hype as usual, but dead to me too.

When school is done, I meet Mike and we walk into the crowd of other dismissed kids acting wild. I watch this kid Benny smack this kid Jonah's neck real hard.

"NECK!" Benny yells.

Heads point and laugh at how Jonah got necked.

I wish somebody would neck me because then maybe I could explode and break on somebody, break anything.

Mike looks in my face. He scans it like he sees something he never saw before. "Bryan, you good?"

"Why?"

"You look kind of wild like your pops when he's OD pissed or amped."

I say my next words and it feels like some voice outside of me speaks. "My dad is locked up."

His face drops and he stops walking. "Word?"

"Word. He didn't come home last night," I say. "He was with that snake Alex." I point at a random building. "You think we could get on that building's roof?"

"Why?"

I'm already walking to that building.

Mike catches up and grabs my forearm. "Stop. Let's talk about your dad some—"

I snatch my arm. "You coming to the roof? Or staying?"

"Okay. Coming."

In the elevator ride up, he doesn't try speaking to me and I like that. I can't think straight so I can't talk straight.

Next thing you know, we're on the roof of some building and I have no problem leaning over the edge of the wall. I watch the insect-size cars and people move around below. I feel monster big.

I scoop up a handful of gravel and jiggle it in my palm. I like the sound and feel of the stones clinking sharp in my hand.

"You think I could hit that car?" I ask.

Mike isn't in the mood. "Why you not letting me know more about your pops?"

I point. "That brown car right there."

And before Mike can get his next word out, a man down on the street spots me. "Hey!" he yells. "There's a kid on the roof!"

Mike yanks me with all his strength down and out of sight. "You crazy?" He looks dead in my eye. "What the heck is wrong with you?"

"What?"

"Bruh," he says, "if you throw a rock, don't be Stuck On Stupid. Throw, then duck fast."

"I know," I tell Mike real fast. "I'm just so hyped up with this Pa stuff. I don't even know if I was gonna throw a rock. But you look like you get this release when you throw them and I guess I was thinking I might feel that too—"

"I feel you," he interrupts. "There's this rush, this release, and a little like I'm getting back at the world. But you know what would mess that all up? If we get busted. Let's dip."

CHAPTER 17

When we're off the roof and outside, I look across the street and see the man who spotted me talking to Ma's friend Mina—the one who runs gossip to her. Did the old dude tell Mina that a boy was on the roof? Will she think I'm that boy? We move fast and I cover my face with my hand like I'm whispering something to Mike, hoping she doesn't see me.

As we head to my block, Mike says something I never knew. "My pops. My pops be in and out. Like yours. You know what I'm saying?"

I nod to let him keep talking because I'm curious about his dad. But when he doesn't say anything, I ask, "You want to say more?"

As soon as I say that, Mike's face tightens.

"Nah."

It's weird how he shut down, like he regrets even bringing it up.

Something else is weird. Even though Pa is locked up, I expect him to be here as we approach his corner. Like he's supposed to be free. It might be silly. But I feel that.

Nicholas, the cool older dark-skinned dude with the all-white hair, calls to me. "You looking more like your pops every day." He wraps an arm around my shoulder and whispers in my ear on the low, "*You heard anything from him? How's he doing?*"

Another friend of Pa's yells, "Little Joe!"

"Oye! Joelito!" Another winks at me.

Soon, almost every guy is calling me a mini-me of Pa, and my heart speeds up and it makes me feel good.

"Same slim build as Joe," Nicholas says, all proud like I'm his son.

I look up and smile at him.

"Same hair and cheeks too," Pito says. I remember when he told Pa he'd look out for me and wouldn't let anybody mess with me. Now he shakes my hand and slips me a folded five-dollar bill.

And as my heart beats faster and harder with the rhythm of the action of Pa's friends, showing me love and comparing me with him, another voice fires off: "Same eyes."

Same eyes. Same eyes. Same eyes.

Me and Mike nod and leave and are halfway down the block when I check out our reflection in the windows we pass.

Mike looks like Mike.

But me . . . my eyes . . .

For the first time, I'll admit that my eyes look like Pa's when he has that hyped, intense stare. It usually scares me when Ava or Ma says my eyes look like his, but now, Pa's eyes on my face looking back at me shoots other feelings through me. It makes me feel like I can handle anything and man up while Pa's locked up.

Yeah, I tell myself, *you have Pa's eyes.* I cock my shoulders back, push out my chest a little, and ball my hands into fists.

Back home, me and Mike sit on my stoop.

"Don't you want to do something?" he asks. "Like really *do* something?"

Since I fiend for life to be different, I ask, "Like?"

I don't see it coming when Mike mentions cutting school again. Maybe because he dropped it for so long.

"Hold up," I say.

I come back with Ma's notebook where she writes down recipes and my composition notebook. I start trying to copy her handwriting.

Mike watches me, smiling. "It almost looks the same. You'll be a pro in no time. Keep going."

• • •

That night, I can't sleep.

I get out of bed and go to my T-shirt drawer. I pull out a photo of Pa that I've had since I was little. And I start missing him so bad, I get mad.

I put the photo back and sit on my bed.

I feel all this stuff building up in me. Like I need to do something. Like I can't think straight. My knee gets jumpy. I go unzip the secret pocket in my book bag. I pull out and unfold the paper that I tore from my notebook where I practiced Ma's handwriting. It has everything from imitations of her signature to whole sentences. I'm getting the hang of Ma's really artsy loops in her lowercase *j*'s, *g*'s, *p*'s, *f*'s, *q*'s, and *y*'s. I start feeling impressed because Mike said I'll be a pro soon.

But that's not the only thing I feel looking at this paper with my ma's handwriting in my handwriting. The other thing I feel is a question. I wonder, *Are you really doing this?*

And that question stays on my brain.

CHAPTER 18

Sunday night, me and Mike sit side by side on my bed and compare drawings we just finished.

He shows me his. "What you think?"

"I like the details you put in Darth Vader's outfit," I say. "And bust how you got Kylo Ren coming out of Darth Vader's shadow! Kid, this is bananas! Like, this looks *real*. In that first movie, they set it up like Kylo Ren is the new Vader. It'd be crazy if we had some of those expensive color art pens or pencils that our school has. You know how sick this'll be if you colored in these lightsabers?"

I swear, his drawing is so good that I can hear Darth Vader's and Kylo Ren's voices in my head. I hear their lightsabers pulsing and throbbing those sword-fighting sounds.

"Let me see yours," Mike asks about my drawing.

I don't want to show him mine because I didn't go all out. But I show him.

He moves his hand across my drawing and big-ups my Flash. "That's wavy. You got the Flash moving so fast, parts of him are almost invisible."

I start thinking my drawing might not be as bad as I thought.

Mike's hand moves across my drawing to another part. "*Word?* Son, you draw Transformers?" He taps Bumblebee. "*Teach me* how to draw him."

I give him a look. Is he for real? His drawings are *way* past mine. I try reading his face but can't tell if he's seriously feeling my art. But his face looks like he means it.

Sometimes, this is how it is with Mike, and it's the part that keeps me being friends with him. I could be feeling down and dude says something that gets me up. I know my drawing isn't dip, but he's making me feel like I'm on his level.

We talk about our drawings some more, then Mike switches topics, lowering his voice to almost a whisper. "So, you got your moms's handwriting yet?"

I jump up, go outside my room, come back with her shopping list, copy part of it, and hand it to him.

He holds the list. He's impressed.

"Do *eggs*." He hands me back the copy paper. "You said her *g*'s were hard."

I bust that out and hand it back to him.

"I can't even tell the difference," he says, straining to find one.

He gets up and pulls a paper out of his book bag. "Now, write one of these and you won't have to go to school."

I take it from him. It reads:

To Whom It May Concern:

*Please excuse my son Mike from school this Tuesday.
I am taking him to a doctor's appointment.*

*Sincerely,
Nancy Freedman*

"You wrote this?" I ask. "Or your moms? Because this looks *nothing* like your handwriting."

"This Tuesday they're releasing the newest *X-Men* comic," Mike says. "That joint'll be sold out if we wait until dismissal to cop that. I'm hitting that Carroll Gardens comic store in the morning. You should come."

I look back at him. "How you use this note?"

"Just show your homeroom teacher," he says. "Ask her to tell your other teachers that you'll be out. If it's her telling them, they'll believe it. Adults believe adults. But if you show every teacher your note, you killed it. That's at least five teachers seeing the handwriting and five chances for someone to spot it's not real. Five chances to get caught."

This feeling rushes through me. I can't tell if it's excitement, nervousness, or what.

"So?" he presses me.

"Yo, I can't get busted, bruh."

"You won't. *Never. Never* has a teacher busted me. Just give it to your homeroom teacher at the end of the day," Mike says.

"At the end of the day, teachers are mad faded and tired. They don't even want to deal with us."

He takes that fake note from his moms and acts it out. "I go up to the teacher like this and say, 'Oh, I forgot to give this to you,' and they barely look at it. One look, they're, like, 'Fine.' Most teachers don't even keep the note. They write down somewhere that I'll be absent and hand my note right back to me. Then, I take it and burn it or rip it up so my moms won't find it."

"This Tuesday?" I ask Mike.

"This Tuesday. *Just* this Tuesday."

I stand, not even sure that I want to do this, but I grab another sheet of paper and sit back down. "Give me that shopping list. And your note."

He does, then grabs his *Star Wars* drawing and goes back to adding details.

I copy word for word what his note says. But I sign it with my moms's name.

Then I show him.

He smiles wide like it's Christmas. "You know, you not going to believe how much fun we'll have on Tuesday."

• • •

It's five minutes till class ends. I stand and feel my knees get weak a little. My heart beats faster and harder. My stomach flips from nervousness. I swallow hard and pretend I'm Mike.

"Excuse me, Ms. Whitman."

Her back is to me as she packs up her expensive-looking

brown leather bag. Ms. Whitman's long blond hair is in a bun and bobs up and down.

"Yes?" She doesn't even turn around.

"My mother told me to give you this."

Ms. Whitman holds the note close to her glasses.

I swear every second she reads my note, my heart beats faster and faster. It's beating as fast as the race car tires blur in those Fast and Furious movies.

She hums as she reads. "Mm-mmm."

I feel my heart stop.

"Mmm. Okay. Tell your mother thank you for letting me know."

"Okay." I turn to leave, not believing it just worked. I feel the rush I feel when I play tag and shake off whoever is "it."

"Um . . . Bryan." Her voice hits my back like an arrow, and my heart stops again. I feel caught.

"Yes?"

"Here. Take this letter back. I'll write myself a reminder on a Post-it."

WHOA to the *WHOA*!

CHAPTER 19

The next morning, we link up behind the check cashing spot near the highway that splits our project from the rich, mostly white neighborhood next to us.

Me and Mike don't even speak. We fist-bump, then jaywalk across the highway.

I feel like I'm in a *Ms. Pac-Man* video game because I dodge speeding cars at the right time the way I dodge ghosts in the game.

Safe on the street, I expect to dip left and uphill mad blocks to the comic store in Carroll Gardens. Mike goes right.

"It's too far to walk," he says. "Let's take the train."

"I'm broke."

"It's cool. I got it."

I look surprised at him.

I like that he saved enough for me to ride the train too— that's good looking out and what a brother would do.

I think back to times he didn't share with me and I jumped to feeling that he was grimy and not acting like a brother. Now he's here acting this way and I'm the one feeling grimy.

• • •

In the train station, Mike moves like a snake, slithering quick through the crowd toward the turnstiles. There, he waves me over.

I'm confused.

"You see five-oh?" he whispers.

I check. "Nah," I whisper back. "Why we checking for cops?"

Mike ducks under a turnstile and races up the steps.

"PAY YOUR FARE!" the teller's voice yells through the microphone in the MetroCard booth. It sounds extra scary because it's all metallic, like Darth Vader's voice.

I watch Mike's sneakers race up the stairs and out of sight.

I'm so scared and don't know what to do. My eyes shoot everywhere. But the people coming in and out of the station don't know or don't care about what Mike just did. Even the teller in the booth is back to handling money and MetroCards.

I'm so Stuck On Stupid! I have to make a move.

I jet to a turnstile and duck under.

"PAY YOUR FARE!" the teller's scary Darth Vader voice barks at me as I race up two steps at a time.

Everywhere on my body, I sweat.

I'm out of breath.

I'm OD amped from what just happened. OD scared a cop will pop out of somewhere and arrest me when I turn the next corner.

When I finally get to the platform, I see Mike chilling against a pole like he did nothing.

I'm so tight I want to push him off the platform onto the

79

train tracks. But I'm also so out of breath and relieved no cops are around that I hunch forward and wipe my T-shirt bottom across my sweaty forehead.

I deep-breathe over and over to get myself together.

Mike comes and rests a hand on my shoulder. "Crazy, right?"

I hear the smile in his voice. I also hear all the curse words in my head that I want to explode on him. Before I can say or do anything, I feel the platform under my kicks rumble and the train coming.

"C'mon," he says.

I look up and see the small light in front of the train grow bigger and brighter as it approaches.

Then I feel Mike's arm scoop under mine to move me along.

"You have to tell me next time before you pull some stupidness like that," I tell Mike.

"I didn't tell you," he whispers, "because I didn't even know I would do that." He pulls out a bunch of bills from his pocket. I see a five, a ten, and a few singles. "I *have* loot. But tell me what we did wasn't more fun."

I have questions I should ask. *Were you planning to do this? Why you look so relaxed hopping that turnstile? What do you think would've happened if cops caught us?*

But I don't ask. Those questions might make me look soft.

Boop! Boop! The train's door closes behind us.

Our train pulls out, turns, then all this sunlight busts into the windows opposite of us.

I lean the back of my head against the window. *Wow.* The Freedom Tower is on the right, standing high above my pip-

80

squeak projects buildings, which are on the left. In between my projects and the Freedom Tower is my school. The kids in my class are probably doing our Do Now right now. Or Ms. Cransfeld is telling kids something we probably won't remember. I don't know what is going on in class right now but I do know that as much as I'm tight at Mike for pulling that turnstile stunt, I know he's right.

What we just did was crazy. And fun.

Real quick, the Manhattan skyline starts disappearing out of sight as our train sinks. We dive into a tunnel.

Mike taps me. "Come look."

I follow him, weaving through the crowd of people. Soon, we get to the front of the train and there is this little window at the door of the operator's booth. Mike looks, then steps out of the way to let me. I peek in and it's bananas.

I can see the operator drive the train, and I can see ahead of the train onto the tracks as we go in the tunnel.

The tunnel is dark. It's scary. It's dope.

"Yooooo," I say to Mike.

"It feels like you flying through the tunnel," he tells me. "Right?"

That's the exact feeling. "Word."

CHAPTER 20

"Hey, Rob." The guy behind the counter of the comic store calls Mike the wrong name but treats Mike like he's used to seeing him. "Who is your friend?"

I expect Mike to call me his brother but he goes with what the cashier said. "This is my friend Ray."

I feel like this is a moment to copycat Mike so I nod like my name is Ray, follow Mike into an aisle, and pull a comic off a shelf like he does.

We're next to each other, flipping pages, and pretty far from the cashier. I whisper to Mike, "Rob? Ray?"

He puts a finger over his lips. "*Later.*"

First, we're standing. Next, we're sitting crisscross-applesauce. Then, we're standing again. In total? We hang in the store enough to read maybe ten comics apiece. Maybe an hour passes.

Then Mike grabs the newest *X-Men* comic that he came for and a few others. He pays and we head outside.

"Now what?" I ask.

"Now we hit somewhere to chill where five-oh won't bug us."

"The park?" I ask.

"Um? *Hello?*" He sounds like he's talking down to me like I'm an idiot. "If you a cop looking for kids cutting school, where's the first place you'd look?"

"A park."

"That's why we going to Starbucks." He points up the block to a Starbucks.

"Cops drink coffee," I say, trying to talk down to him, and I shoot him a look like, *Who's the idiot now, huh?*

"True," Mike says, "but I got this."

There he goes again saying that. *I got this.*

I don't trust him because the last time he said that he meant something else.

"Nah." I stop walking. "What do you mean, 'I got this'?"

Mike huffs and looks me up and down like I'm softer than soft, like I'm being a baby.

He smirks, shakes his head, then leaves for Starbucks.

I feel so far away from where I should be. It might sound silly, but I feel far away from who I am.

I should be in school, but I followed Mike here. I shouldn't have hopped a turnstile, but I followed him and did. I watch him walk off and see that he doesn't turn around. He *knows* that I'll follow him. Because I have to. I have no train money to ride home. Even if I did have money, I've never ridden the train by myself.

Mike calls all the shots, knows it, and has me kissing his butt.

I feel myself getting tight and something in me wants

to explode. I wish I could catch up to him and throw him a beating.

But then what? I'd still be stuck in a new neighborhood without a dime or a clue to get home.

I catch up to him and follow him into Starbucks.

He looks around like he's searching for something. "There." He points at grown-ups who could pass for our family. He leans in and whispers, "Sit kind of close to them but not close enough to freak them out. If cops walk in, they won't question us because they'll assume we're with them."

We do that, and as soon as we're in seats, I lean in and he leans in too.

I ask, "Why you call me Ray back there? Why you Rob?"

Mike says, "Don't ever give your real name if you cut school. Heads know who you are, then soon your moms knows what you did. So you Ray and I'm Rob. Want a coffee, *Ray*? My treat."

I nod. I never had Starbucks before.

It smells good.

He hands me his comics and heads to the cashier.

When he brings me my cup, I sip and feel grown drinking it because only grown-ups are here drinking coffee.

For the rest of our time in Starbucks, we call each other Rob and Ray.

At first, I hate it.

After a few sips, I guess my new name isn't so bad. Batman is Bruce Wayne. Power Man is Luke Cage. Heroes have two different identities. Mike is Rob. I'm Ray.

Sitting and reading with chill people and listening to music in this Starbucks reminds me of when Ma takes me out of the projects for some "us time."

We both like to do exactly this, except no coffee.

This is our thing: chilling and being peaceful.

The people sitting in here being quiet and calm make me wonder—are they always like this? What other places do they go to be chill when they leave here?

It feels like my projects' drama doesn't even exist. So when the people next to us who look like family stand and leave, I feel sad.

"Now what?" I ask Mike.

"Over there." He nods at a man and woman who can pass for family.

Mike has to tell me "Be smooth about it," because I grab the comics and start cleaning up our table too quick. He reminds me to head over there without being obvious.

We do. And maybe an hour later, we do it again. And when we can't hop from table to table anymore, he says we're getting food and going back to our projects to find a roof to stay on until school is dismissed.

I think that sounds boring but it isn't. The feeling we have in Starbucks—we just bring that to the roof. We sit, we read, we snack, we draw, and it's chill. There is no coffee. There is no music. But it's chill. And there is no rock throwing.

At one point, I look at Mike, and I think something I'd never tell him because it sounds soft. I think that I'm lucky that Pa left Mike for me. Pa couldn't introduce me to my three real brothers, but he introduced me to him and he feels almost like a real brother. Doing this up here on the roof feels like what brothers would do.

CHAPTER 21

We wait a few days to cut school again.

The second time we cut we go back to the train station. This time I follow Mike more smoothly.

Soon, we're walking to the last car.

"Don't get on," he tells me.

"But I thought we riding it downtown," I say.

"We. Are. Just listen and don't get on."

I try to figure out what he's up to. I watch people get off and on the train. I hear the recorded man's voice say, "Stand clear of the closing doors, please." I hear the BOOP! BOOP! letting everyone know the doors are shutting. I watch them shut.

I ask, "How we riding this train if—"

Mike goes to the back of the outside of the train and starts climbing on! First, he stretches to reach for these handles. Then, one of his feet leaves the platform. Then, his other foot. Now, he's completely on the outside of the back of the train. My eyes shoot down to the track. Nothing is between him and that five-, six-foot drop.

"Climb on!" He snaps me out of my thoughts.

I step back on reflex. "Nah."

The train huffs, shakes, and inches forward.

"Stupid!" he barks at me. "Once this train moves, you ain't getting on! *GET! ON!*"

And . . .

. . . I . . .

. . . stop thinking.

I. Do. What. He. Did.

First, I reach for one of those free handles I saw him grab. My heart beats so hard. The train picks up speed.

Then, real quick, I swing both of my feet off the platform. I can feel my hands sweat from my nervousness and I try gripping the handle harder, but my hands are too slick from sweat. I'm afraid I'll lose my grip once the train zooms fast. And the train is zooming, faster and faster.

My eyes shoot down to the track.

I'm completely on the outside of the back of the train and there's a five-, six-foot drop to the tracks. The tracks are a blur. I look at the platform. Everything on it is a blur too. That's how fast the train speeds. Nothing is between me and the tracks. Nothing can catch me if I fall. I look at my sweaty, slippery hands and hold on for my life.

I have all these scared feelings and I'm bugging out.

Then I look at Mike and he has the biggest smile.

He yells something at me, and I think it's WOO-HOO! but I can't hear nothing with all this outside train noise hurting my ears.

But his face and eyes.

This is the happiest I've ever seen him.

Until his face disappears as our train zooms into the tunnel.

• • •

For a few seconds, everything is pitch-black. Then my eyes adjust. So does my hearing.

Bright white sparks like fireworks spark on the train's rails.

There is a rhythm to those sparks.

One, two, three: *CRAAACK!*

One, two: *CRAAACK! CRAAACK!*

One, two, three, four: *CRAAACK!*

Sometimes, the rhythm is off.

It's like I'm hypnotized and I keep staring at the sparks behind me when I should focus on holding on. I readjust my grip.

The sparks of light reveal flashes of graffiti and piles of trash along paths of the tunnel. It all makes it feel like I'm in a dark underground fantasy world of monsters, trolls, demons, and half-human, half-animal creatures from comics. A world I'm glad I'm not walking through.

The outline of Mike's smiling face flashes at me.

"WOO-HOOOO!" I yell at him, knowing he probably can't hear me over the tunnel and train sounds. But I yell again anyway. "THIS IS CRAAAAAAAZEEEEEEEE!!!"

• • •

When the train stops in the next station, Mike motions for me to rush onto the platform.

I start but first peek real slow up and down the platform to see if grown-ups or cops will bust me climbing off the train's back.

"Hurry up!" Mike's elbow shoves my back over and over. "Get off!"

"STOP! I don't want to get caught."

"Then I'm climbing over you!"

I scoot onto the platform. He does too.

"Act normal," he says on the DL, "but walk quicker to blend in with heads going upstairs."

Me and him catch up and flow with people until we're near the MetroCard booth.

I'm already jumpy, but then get jumpier because I swear that the booth worker looks dead at us. I want to turn around and go back downstairs. "She looking here?"

"Who?" Mike asks.

"The lady in the booth," I tell him.

"You bugging."

When we pass the booth worker and she says nothing, I feel my whole everything relax.

Soon, we're upstairs, outside, and Mike congratulates me.

"You're what's up, bruh! Nobody soft would ride outside a train like that! C'mere. You gangsta."

He wraps an arm around my neck and noogies my head with his knuckle.

It feels so good getting props from him that I decide not to say half of what I want! Like, *You almost got us killed.* Like, *A few times I almost lost my grip.* Instead, I say, "You did that before?"

"Train-surfing," he says, like everyone but me knows what

that means. "I *been* doing that. That's why I said trust me. You wouldn't get hurt."

Whatevs. What would he've done if I fell off the train? Dive onto the tracks like he could fly and scoop me up?

I'm so shook from train-surfing and so not believing that we just did that that I'm quiet while we walk the block. I can't explain it, but my feet feel funny standing on solid ground. After watching the train's tracks blur real fast under my feet, it feels like the ground should be moving. I look around at people walk or jog and everyone looks . . . slow. Even fast passing cars look slow.

This past summer, Ma took me to Luna Park on Coney Island and I rode this roller coaster. It moved so fast that I got off and wanted to get on again and again and again and . . . But Ma had money for just one ride. Train-surfing is free. I could train-surf all day if I wasn't so scared of falling and dying.

"You ever get hurt train-surfing?" I ask Mike.

"You serious? I'm here, ain't I?"

• • •

Later, at night, me and Mike chill in my room. We watch *The Flash* on the CW.

We're on the edge of my bed, not making a sound and not moving a muscle. It's like we don't breathe when Flash is on because this show is *that* fuego.

Right now, Flash faces off with an evil speedster, the Reverse Flash. Zoom is another evil speedster that Flash sometimes has to stop.

Flash is the man. No doubt.

I wish I could move like him. Maaan, the stuff I *would do*!

Flash and Reverse Flash stare at each other for a second, but it feels mad long. Then *CRAAAACK!* Electric sparks fly off Reverse Flash, and he disappears out of sight. He is a bolt of red light blurring faster than fast through the city. Flash's body crackles a blinding electric spark, and soon, he's a yellow blur right behind Reverse Flash. All these sparks spark off them as their arms and legs blur the way things blurred when we train-surfed.

"You see those sparks?" I point at the TV screen.

"Yeah."

"That's how that train track lit up today."

"Word." Mike grins. "I never put that together."

"That's me and you, bruh." I nod at Flash. "We were moving like Flash."

He gets competitive for no reason. "But in a real race, I'd body you."

"You killed it. I'm just having fun, comparing."

He stays competitive and the look on his face matches Reverse Flash on TV. His smile reminds me of when I waxed him in *Ms. Pac-Man* at the arcade. Back then, I wasn't sure if he was fake-smiling, but right now, I'm sure he is. He's all teeth with serious eyes. He says, "Yeah, Bryan, I know you just comparing us to the show. But you know you dumb slow, right? And I'd body you in a race?"

I feel myself get annoyed. I practice Ma's advice. I take a

deep breath and change the subject. "How much electricity was in that train track?"

"More than six hundred volts." He chuckles. "I could picture you touching it and it frying you. Zaap." He laughs at his wack joke. "Ha! You'd be Kentucky Fried Bryan. *Zaaaap.*"

I deep-breathe again.

I stand and grab my remote and crank up the volume to *The Flash.*

CHAPTER 22

Right after we play handball the next afternoon, me and Mike sit on the sidelines and kind of watch some men play. He dribbles the handball between his legs.

"Bryan," he says, "let's play You Get Annoyed When . . ."

"I don't know how to play."

"I'll go first. I say, 'You get annoyed when . . . ,' then you finish my sentence with something that annoys you. You start it off, and I'll tell you what annoys me."

"You get annoyed when . . ."

Mike says, "When I'm on a toilet and I think the stall door is locked, then someone opens it and catches me there with my pants down. You get annoyed when . . ."

"The milk carton says the milk is good, then I sip and it's sour," I say. "You get annoyed when . . ."

Mike stops dribbling the handball. "Let's switch it up. I'll say, 'You get annoyed when . . . ,' then I'll add a subject like 'Gross,' 'Serious,' or 'Funny,' and you say something gross or serious that annoys you. Bet?"

I shrug. "Go."

He says, "You get annoyed when . . . FUNNY!"

"When cross-eyed dudes try to be bullies. Cross-eyed dudes can't even see who they bullying. Once, this cross-eyed dude tried to bully me and I ran left. Dude didn't even know where to look. Anyways, you get annoyed when . . . GROSS."

Mike makes a disgusted face. "When people spit on handrails in staircases. Once, I put my hand on a rail, and the eggiest glob of spit smeared all over my palm. Yuck! You get annoyed when . . . SERIOUS."

"When I'm home and everybody is in my space."

He squeezes the handball in his hand and looks at it, flattening it. He says, "Yo, wanna play another game?"

"Sure."

"Same game but I'll say, 'You get hyped when . . . ,' then you'll say something that you think is dope."

"Go first."

Mike says, "You get hyped when . . ."

"When I draw a superhero and it looks almost like the comic. You get hyped when—"

We get interrupted by rap beats so loud it feels like a block party just drove onto our street. Mike's head swivels so much to see where the music comes from that he looks like an owl I saw on TV that made its head do a complete three-sixty turn. It's a black Jeep with tinted windows like the whips Jay-Z and famous people get driven in. As it passes by us, Mike's eyes are so wide he looks hypnotized.

He finally responds to my asking him what gets him hyped. He says, "I get hyped when I see fat whips like that. Yo, you saw those rims?!"

I'm not into cars like that so I change the subject. "Want to play handball some more?"

"Nah."

"Then can I borrow the ball to practice?"

He makes a stingy face and says, "Get your own ball." Then, under his breath, "People never have their own stuff. Gotta beg me for what's mine."

What is he even talking about? All the times I've shared with him? And he's making a huge deal of me asking for his handball for like five minutes?

I hate when he acts like this.

• • •

When I walk in our living room, Ava's watching TV.

"Where's Ma?" I ask.

Ava waves at Ma's bedroom without looking away from the TV like drama is about to pop off.

On Ava's show, one guy acts grimy to another guy.

"Whoa!" I say. "He's violating. Why?"

"Shhh. Watch and stop asking questions." Ava scoots over on the couch.

I watch and see a neighborhood like ours, and the characters remind me of people out here. And it's crazy timing because I just came from Mike acting foul and not knowing how to respond and the same kind of stuff is happening on this show.

"Can you believe this?" Ava asks.

I can't take my eyes off the screen so I just give a thumbs-up. "Yeah."

When the show ends, Ava does something unexpected. She sits crisscross-applesauce facing me and talks to me like she'd kick it with a tight friend. "It's so real," she says. "Right?"

I feel like telling her how *really* real it is for me—that Mike can be as grimy as the dude on the show. But I don't for a few reasons. First, Ava thinks Mike is cool. Plus, I like how me and her are getting along and I don't want to kill it. So, instead, I ask, "Why you into this show?"

"This shows is facts." She starts listing on fingers. "First, it teaches you to always use your head. Second, just because people bug out doesn't make them all bad. Also, if you cut someone off who is mostly good to you, you won't have them as backup when you need it. Fourth, always talk it out if you can."

I sit there, connecting in my head what Ava says to Mike and I realize she's right, including the part about talking things out. But I don't even know what to say to him when he flips moods on me. I ask, "You learned stuff from this show you use?"

"Definitely. So, in this show, some guys from the other record company came to jump the main character. They approached him on the street thinking he was alone, and he was, but he pointed up the block at this group of guys and fronted to be with them. The troublemakers left him alone. That's a trick I used on this girl Maddie. She and her girls tried to mess with me as I passed. 'Oh, you think you cute. You think you're all

97

that,' she said to me. I looked her right in the eye and pretended like the character in the show. 'Yeah,' I told her. 'And you know who else thinks I am?' I pointed up the block at some girls our age who I know Maddie isn't cool with. 'Karina, Stephanie, Lizbeth, and all them.' And just like that, Maddie started acting all nice and let me pass."

"That was smooth," I tell Ava.

She soft-punches my knee. "Right? You should watch this some more with me."

CHAPTER 23

At dismissal the next day, I don't wait for Mike on our school's corner. I just want to go to Ma's job. Solo. That's it. That's how I feel.

"Bryan?"

I surprise Ma from behind with a hug.

Ma's my heart. The way she strokes my head and cheek. The way she smells the same good smell. The way she hugs me back and her hug makes me not want to leave her. I start to feel like I want to tell her so much ill stuff I've done with Mike. But if I told her, it'd be a wrap. She'd ground me for half the stuff me and him been into. She'd kill me for the other half of stuff we did.

"Where is Mike?" she asks.

"I just want to do homework alone in my office."

"Okay." She pats my shoulder. "Go ahead."

I go into my office, shrug off my book bag, grab my clipboard off my file cabinet, sit in my desk-chair, and look at my clipboard's notes. My eyes move down the page of what I wrote, but I'm not really reading. I'm just feeling this quiet. I'm feeling being alone.

I look at Ma for a second. Maybe I can tell her some things about Mike. Some things about me.

"Ma?" I call her.

She comes to me. "What's up, baby?"

"Since you not busy, want to sit in my office?"

Then, out of nowhere, it gets busy. This boy who looks my age with a grown man and woman appear at Ma's desk.

I tell Ma, "They looking for you?"

Ma turns to them and jumps straight into helping them. She pauses. "Bryan, can you come help me out?"

"Sure."

Ma introduces me and the boy. "This is Kamau. Kamau, this is my son, Bryan."

We nod hi.

"Bryan," Ma asks, "can Kamau do his homework with you while his parents and I go over some paperwork?"

I nod at Kamau to follow me. His gear isn't like the kids from my projects. Or from any of the places me and Mike visited lately. He looks broke like his fam has even less money than we have when we struggle-struggle. As we head into my office, I ask him, "You live out here?"

He doesn't speak. He just stares at the floor and shakes his head. Maybe he's shy.

I wave at a foldable metal chair for him to sit and I go sit in mine. I slide my book bag to my feet, unzip it, and start pulling out my schoolbooks and stuff to get ready to do my homework.

As I start stacking that on my desk, Kamau sits straight up. His eyes get all lit and curious and glued to a comic sticking out my pile of schoolbooks.

"I like that comic." His accent isn't from here. He sounds Jamaican or something.

"This?" I hand him my *Fantastic Four* comic.

He takes it and looks through it mad quiet. He doesn't look like he could be me or Mike's brother, but his eyes are the way ours used to look when we spent hours hypnotized by comics.

"Who would you be?" I ask.

He looks at me, confused.

"Like which of the Fantastic Four would you be?"

"The Human Torch." His accent isn't Jamaican. I know because the lunch lady at school is Jamaican and they sound different.

"Where you from? You sound like you speak another language."

"I'm African. From Kenya."

"Word? For real, for real?!"

He looks at me like I'm clowning him.

"Nah, I mean that's wavy you African. I mean cool. You know this comic?" I shuffle through my stuff, then find it. "This is Black Panther. He's African. Like you."

Kamau takes it into his hands. He doesn't know *Black Panther*.

He flips through it like he is in heaven.

"Who would you be?" he asks me.

"Who what?"

He chuckles. "If you were a Fantastic Four."

"Oh. Like you. I'd be the Human Torch. Like, who else on that team is better, y'feel me?"

Right now, I notice two things.

First, this is the first time I hit it off with another kid about comics since me and Mike. Mad heads know comics, but they don't get amped the way me and Mike get amped. Clicking with Kamau is rare: the way we jump straight into comics like this.

The second thing I notice is that girl Melanie from my school is in here with her parents. They seem to be just dropping off some big, closed yellow envelope and chatting. I don't know how long she's been watching me with Kamau, but this time I can tell she's happy with what she sees. She smiles and waves like it's cool I'm being cool with Kamau.

I wave back. This is way better than the last time she saw me and shot me a disgusted look like I was an idiot for being with Mike as he kept smacking James.

If that's not cool enough, me and Kamau go back to talking about how tight it'd be to fly above skyscrapers and shoot flames from our hands like Human Torch.

"Flame on!" we say at the same time.

"How hot do you think he gets?" Kamau asks.

We geek out on that.

Then I ask, "Do you think he could melt Colossus from *X-Men*?"

We bug for a while on that.

"Or that metal that makes up Wolverine's claws and skeleton?" Kamau asks. "The same metal in Captain America's shield, do you think he could melt that?"

Man! Me and this dude have fun like me and Mike before Mike turned . . .

"You moving out here?" I ask. I hope so.

"No," he says. "My parents want your mom to help us get an apartment in another neighborhood where my dad starts a job."

"Oh." I try fronting like I'm not disappointed.

"Anyways," I bring the conversation back to the Human Torch. "What if Iceman from the *X-Men* and the Human Torch faced off? Who'd win?"

He argues why Iceman has a good chance. Then he argues why the Human Torch might body Iceman.

I'm just eating it up, listening to Kamau.

When I pull some of my drawings of superheroes out of my folder, he gets hyped. He doesn't draw but thinks I got skills.

"How did you do this to Hulk's chest?" He points.

As I answer his question about how I got the shading right on the Hulk's chest, Mike walks in, unfolds a metal chair, and just sits and listens to me and Kamau talk. No hi. He doesn't say what's up to me. He doesn't introduce himself to Kamau. It is mad awkward. He just kind of sits on the edge of us and eavesdrops.

Kamau looks weirded out and shoots me a look like, *You know this guy?*

To make the vibe less awkward, I introduce them. "Kamau, this is Mike."

Mike says mad salty to Kamau, "I'm his brother."

Kamau reaches out to shake his hand.

Mike just looks at it, sucks his teeth, and stares at the floor. "What's good?"

Me and Kamau try going back to what we were discussing but Mike is killing the vibe.

Mike just sits there, staring at his kicks.

Between sentences, me and Kamau keep looking over at Mike like, *What's up with him?*

Soon, Kamau's parents come over.

"Say good-bye to your friend," his father says. "We are leaving."

"Nice to meet you," Kamau tells me. He turns to his parents. "Are we coming back here?"

"No." His mother smiles. "We have everything we need. Everything will happen soon."

Kamau looks happy about that but disappointed me and him won't see each other again.

"Okay, Human Torch," he calls me. "See you."

I call him that back. "Yeah, Human Torch, I'll see you too."

I watch him and his parents leave Ma's job, and as soon as they are out the door, Mike says, "Y'all sounded mad giddy and kiddy." He mocks us, whining, "'Okay, *Human Torch.*'" He lets out one fake laugh. "I felt like I was watching a chick flick and you two were breaking up."

I swear. If we weren't at Ma's job and she and her boss weren't right there across the room, I'd snuff him.

"You calling me soft?" I ask him.

He chuckles. "My bad, Bryan. That's foul of me. For real." He looks sorry. Like he means it. "For real."

I chill a little and remember what Ava said about people who bug out not being all bad.

Mike keeps on. "I'm just tight you flat left me at dismissal."

I relax some more. I feel myself deep-breathing.

I decide to forget how he just acted and accept his apology.

CHAPTER 24

After dinner with Ava and Ma, Ma asks, "Would you both like a surprise?"

Me and Ava nod, then look at each other, wondering what it could be.

Ma goes to the shelves near the TV and reaches behind Ava's and my framed elementary-school graduation photos. "What do you think is behind here?"

Before me and Ava can guess, Ma whips out an envelope. "Your father wrote."

Ava tries to play all cool, but she should see her face. She's lit.

Me too! "What he say?"

Ma sits between us and reads a little, then puts extra on his line, "Give the best daughter and son ever—Ava and Bryan—a big hug and kiss for me. Tell them to keep making me proud. And give them each their photo of me."

I lean in to see where my photo is in the envelope.

Ma reaches in it and pulls ours out.

Ava peeks at mine at the same time I peek at hers.

She says, "I'm putting mine in my mirror," and goes to her room.

I sit with Ma.

I want to tell her stuff but I don't know where to start. I look at my kicks.

"I'm glad Pa wrote," I say.

"Me too."

"So."

"So," she says, smiling. "What's up? What's new?"

"With?"

"I don't know. Anything. Mike?"

I suck my teeth. "Mike?"

"Something happened with him?" Ma asks, real concerned. "I noticed he was acting a little funny at my office."

I shrug. "Yeah. I don't know. He's like two different people. Sometimes."

"How?"

All of a sudden, my words knot in my throat.

Ma sighs. "You know you can tell me anything. What's wrong?"

"Sometimes he really annoys me," I say, starting to talk faster and faster. "He does stuff. Grimy stuff that makes me want to flip on him. One minute, he acts like boom. Then the next, he acts like whoa. He thinks I won't, but I will. And—"

"Are you mad at him?

"Yeah."

"How mad?"

"I don't know. Mad-mad."

"How mad?"

"Sometimes I want to punch him." I look. She doesn't react. I hold my fist up. "Like punch him in the face."

"First, don't use the word *mad*. Animals get mad. Humans get angry," Ma says. "Mike and you are like brothers. Friends get angry at each other. Brothers get really, *really* angry at each other. The way you feel is normal."

I hear that voice in my again. *Yeah, your brother, whatever.* Ma doesn't get it. She doesn't get what's really going on.

"I don't want you fighting him."

"Why?"

"I don't want you getting physical with anyone." Ma pauses, then continues real slow and serious. "When your father gets physical, what happens? Don't answer. Think about it. Think about if he solves a problem or makes a problem bigger."

"Okay, I hear you. But then what do I do? If Mike makes me feel whoa again, I'm supposed to do nothing?"

"Do you want me to talk to him?"

"Noooo. Uh-uh," I tell Ma. "I'll handle it. I'll talk to him the next time something happens. I promise. Just don't go talking to him because he'll think I sent you and he'll think I'm soft."

"Soft?"

"Forget it!" I wave my hands. "Forget I said anything."

"Are you sure?"

"A hundred percent."

CHAPTER 25

I kick it near the water fountain with Big Will. We talk *Ms. Pac-Man* strategy, and I notice Mike not too far off looking at me with a little frown and mean eyes.

I give him a friendly nod and wave for him to come over, but he sucks his teeth and walks off.

"What's up with Mike?" Big Will asks.

I shrug.

"He looks tight that you're hanging with me."

I look at Big Will like *whoa*, because that was my exact thought. "Well, he can be tight. I didn't do anything wrong."

"You should talk to him," Big Will tells me.

"Why?"

He shrugs. "Stop his mood from growing. Keep things cool with him."

I look at Big Will with this feeling I've felt before: He's different, good different. Because me trying to talk to Mike is opposite of how a lot of guys would handle this. Big Will sees things differently, and I think he's right.

At lunchtime, I sit next to Mike.

"When we train-surfing again?" he asks.

"Whenever." I want to train-surf but I feel two ways about it so I tell him, "I don't want to cut school for it. And I don't want to hop turnstiles."

I just want that rush, that release, again.

He nods. "Sure. Let's go Saturday. And it'll be more fun if we bring someone else."

"How about Big Will?"

"Nah." He spits on the floor, sounding jealous.

"C'mon," I say, "he's diesel. Anyone looking for trouble with us in other neighborhoods will back off."

"I just don't like the idea of Big Will."

"Why not?"

Mike shrugs. After a few seconds, he snaps his fingers. "I know exactly who to invite. This kid Kev."

• • •

The next day after school Mike introduces me to Kev. But he calls him "Little Kevin."

Mike points to me. "This is my brother Bryan."

"I know," says Little Kevin.

Little Kevin could not be more opposite of Big Will.

Big Will is in sixth grade, like me, but passes for an eighth grader. Little Kevin is in sixth grade too, but looks like a fourth grader.

Big Will's *hair* has hair. Little Kevin? Does he even have eyebrows?

When Mike cracks a joke, Little Kevin laughs like Mike is the funniest person alive. If Mike stands a certain way, Little

Kevin copycats him. It's mad annoying and reminds me of me when I first thought Mike was the man.

Other ways that Big Will and Little Kevin are opposite: Big Will isn't fazed by dip dudes rocking bling or pushing fat whips. When we talk and they roll by, Big Will's eyes stay on me and he keeps up the conversation. Not Little Kevin. As me, him, and Mike talk, a real loud car drives up our block, blasting music and revving its motor. Yo, I swear, Mike and Little Kevin act like robots who had their same button pushed—they stop talking and become hypnotized by the car. And as soon as it disappears, they say the same thing. "That car was sick. Imagine that was ours."

Little Kevin hits Mike with a list of questions. "What would your rims look like? Would they spin backward? And what about your windows? Tinted like that SUV? Or darker because that's wavier?"

Ugh. Little Kevin's voice comes out sounding as if he thinks Mike's the biggest, smartest person ever and I sort of can't stand it. Maybe because I know more about Mike now and know he's not perfect.

Mike reacts to Little Kevin like Mike is some superstar, giving an autograph to a thirsty fan. He puts his hand on Little Kevin's shoulder like Little Kevin is dumb and needs to be schooled. "Rims would be flavor but super-dark tints don't matter. What you *first* need is an ill sound system."

"Yeah but—" Little Kevin tries talking back.

"But nothing," Mike interrupts him.

Little Kevin tries talking back again. "Yeah, but—"

"BUT *you* don't know." Mike shuts him down again.

I can tell Mike likes acting like he has all the answers and knows everything about everything.

Finally, Little Kevin gets it and changes the subject. "So you told me about train-surfing. When you going train-surfing next?" he asks.

"Soon," Mike says, and gives Little Kevin that Steve Harvey fake-snake smile, which gives me a bad feeling about Little Kevin coming with us.

CHAPTER 26

On Tuesday, me and Mike run into Little Kevin near this brownstone building where some older swagged-out high school guys chill.

"Watch this," Mike says all braggy to Little Kevin.

Mike calls to some of the guys, and they nod and wave back.

I wish I could act out the way Little Kevin's eyes pop when he sees that. "Wow! You know them?" he asks.

Mike wraps an arm around Little Kevin, walks off, and tells him something like he's sharing a secret. I bet he's telling him how he's down with them.

I'm not about to bring Little Kevin to my apartment because I don't know him well, so when Mike turns and says, "Let's head to the pier," I'm happy.

Soon, we're out of our projects, past the stadium's handball courts, then at the piers. There, we dare each other to take off our kicks and walk in the water.

Little Kevin tells Mike he can't swim and asks him a million times, "How deep is it?"

When Mike calls him soft, I get that bad feeling.

Mike goes in on Little Kevin with the disses. *Punk*, *butt*, and other things.

"I'll do it," Little Kevin tells Mike, "if you do."

I watch Little Kevin slowly step in that pier's tide, and he's so scared that he is almost crying. But he does it. He steps in for Mike.

I feel sick to my stomach. I hate seeing how Little Kevin will follow Mike even when it makes no sense.

"You coming in?" Mike asks me.

"Nah," I say, not expecting for that to boom out with so much bass. But it does. I guess my feelings show. "And I'm not soft for not doing it."

I can swim. I just don't feel like it. Maybe I don't want to look like such a follower as Little Kevin, up behind Mike's every move.

I just stare at my kicks on solid ground, then at them two stepping deeper and deeper into the tide as the waves start pounding against their shins. Soon, they're nearly knee deep. I watch Little Kevin fake-laughing.

I watch, as serious as a heart attack.

• • •

The next few days are the same when it comes to me, Mike, and Little Kevin. Mike calls the shots, Little Kevin is too thirsty to follow, and I stop caring that this is how it goes. Why? We do fun stuff, and nobody seems to get hurt. I'm, like, "whatever, whatever" and I'm cool with Mike's ideas.

I'm cool with our fun for another reason: Mike never goes

back to the idea of us train-surfing. I'm thinking, *He's not mentioning it because he doesn't want Little Kevin coming.*

Before, I just had a general bad feeling about Little Kevin train-surfing with us. Now I definitely don't want him coming. The kid has no coordination. When we played handball, Little Kevin couldn't even catch the handball, even when I slow-underhand it to him. So if he can't catch, how will he stay gripping the outside of the train as it zooms faster than the fastest cars? Duh.

He also fell down when we played tag. All Mike had to do was say, "You it," and reach a little toward Little Kevin, and Little Kevin backed up and tripped. He tripped! *Over his own feet!* He fell straight on his butt. Come on. Someone who can't run backward can train-surf? Nah.

Plus, Little Kevin gets too shook too quick too. On Thursday morning, I surprised him as he went from one class to another in our crowded hall. I ran behind and yelled, "BOO!" and he almost jumped out of his body like the scariest-looking zombie in the most haunted house scared him. How is someone who gets that shook that fast ready to handle all that crazy scariness of hanging outside a train above a six-foot drop as the tracks blur under our feet while electricity sparks off the track? *Nuh-uh.*

Then, on Thursday after school when we drop Little Kevin near his stoop, Mike whispers to us both, "Saturday, remember. Train-surfing." Little Kevin gets mad hyped like he's ready; I feel torn and get real quiet.

Mike looks at me funny. "You down?"

I nod. "No doubt. Yeah."

"For real?"

"Yeah! Puh-*leez*, son. You know I'm down to train-surf."

Mike fist-bumps me. "My man!" He taps me and tells me to explain to Little Kevin how crazy fun train-surfing is.

I start doing that, and the whole time I wonder why I don't just say what I really feel. Now it's like *I'm* two people. On the outside, I'm promoting train-surfing so hard. On the inside, I'm like, *Why am I being Mike's hype-man with this?* As I keep telling Little Kevin things, his eyes get wider and wider. He is straight amazed. Now there's no way he's backing out of train-surfing.

When I'm done talking, I want to smack myself for doing the opposite of what I should've.

CHAPTER 27

On Thursday afternoon, I walk into the apartment, and Ma sits at the kitchen table all happy, smirking at me. Ava is on the couch with the same dumb, happy smirk. I'm confused. They look like they have a secret.

'What?" I ask them.

Ma clears her throat.

Then . . . turning the corner . . . from her bedroom . . . is Pa.

HE'S! OUT! OF! JAIL!

PA!!! I want to yell. I want to run and hug him tight. But that's not how we show affection. Plus, the macho way he stands there, all still like a statue, and winks at me with just a tinier version of Ma's happy smirk—it's like he expects a macho reaction from me.

Yeah, he might expect a macho reaction from me, but I can't stop myself from smiling, real big.

Pa comes, rubs my head, and surprises me by pulling me in for a quick hug. I wrap my arms around him, anaconda tight. I feel myself tear up. I press my face into his chest so Ava can't see me cry and call me soft.

I fight hard to hold my tears in. I win. None come out so I pull my face out of his chest for air.

"When you get home?" I ask.

Pa smiles. "While you were at school."

Ma must've been fronting those times she got letters from jail from him and she told us that she didn't know when he was being released.

I ask her, "You knew he'd be out today?"

She just smiles and shrugs.

• • •

For about fifteen minutes, I've been sitting on the edge of Pa and Ma's bed. Usually, Pa acts like I annoy him and tells me to leave his room. Right now, he lets me sit here.

"What was jail like this time?" I ask him.

He does something he's never done before: He answers, a little.

"Jail isn't somewhere you want to go." A frown flashes across Pa's face, then his expression goes back to normal. "Do you like your school rules?"

"Not all of them."

"Why?"

I stare at him, wondering how much to say. He told me I better never curse, so I'm trying to choose the right words. "Some rules are . . . stupid."

Pa nods over and over, slow. "Okay. Now, imagine that your school has a lot more stupid rules and you have to follow every one. Oh, and you sleep at your school. And when you sleep, teachers wake you up, and they make up more stupid rules

you have to follow. You're not fully awake, don't really understand the rules, but you have to follow them."

"Woooooooow." I think about how much that sucks. "Yeah,
but—"

He interrupts me. "Anyway, while I was away, what have
you been up to?"

"Hanging out with Mike."

He smiles. I *knew* it! I knew while Pa was gone he didn't
want me to ditch Mike. I knew I'd make him happy if I stayed
tight with Mike. Since Pa smiled, I throw some extra on that.
"Like every day."

He nods and makes a face like he approves and is happy to
hear that. "Is he a good kid like I thought?"

I want to be honest about sides of Mike he doesn't know. But
I don't know how Pa'll react.

I say, "Yeah. Usually. Why?"

"Good friends. You need good ones. Not backstabbers."

Him saying this makes me wonder why he said that and if
he's changed his mind about that snake Alex.

I'd like to ask him, but all of a sudden, Pa doesn't want to
talk anymore. "Bryan, I'm tired and just want some quiet."

I stand to leave, even though I wish I could stay. Maybe
Pa just wants that feeling I had in Starbucks, of peace, of no
drama. I wish he could see that he could have that feeling with
me and we don't have to talk. We could just sit together and
chill quietly the way me and Ma do.

CHAPTER 28

It's Saturday morning, and me, Mike, and Little Kevin head to the train station.

I try to change Little Kevin's mind. "Kev," I say. "You sure you want to go train-surfing? Check my hands." I show him my calluses. "My hands are tough from handball, and you need strong hands to grip outside the train. Your palms strong? Let me see."

I say this hoping he knows he's weak because he is.

Little Kevin holds his palms up to show me.

Mike steps in between us and puts Little Kevin's hands down. "Kev," he says, "check my hands. You see calluses? No. And my grip is fine."

Mike turns to me, asking, "Bruh. The other day you went on and on about how lit train-surfing is. Now you trying to talk him out of it? Nah. You can't do that. It was lit, *is* lit, and *stays* lit, and you know it." He faces Little Kevin. "Kev, you want to skip train-surfing?"

"Nah."

"Where do you want to go?" Mike asks him.

"Wherever is clever."

Mike smiles. "How about Chinatown?"

Little Kevin shrugs. "Yeah. There or wherever. I'm down."

Mike turns to me. "You can stay if you're scared."

I don't know why I feel like I need to look after Little Kevin. I'm not even sure I like him enough to protect him. But part of me wants to train-surf just to keep him safe.

I tell Mike. "You bugging if you think I'm scared. And you're bugging if you think I'm letting you go without me."

A new worker is in the MetroCard booth at our station. She's busy with paperwork. Outside is as packed as it always is. People move fast in and out of turnstiles and the station.

Little Kevin asks if we have MetroCards or money.

Mike looks at him like he's stupid, but Mike talks to me. "Bryan, tell him we don't pay."

Okay. Back when I told Mike I want to train-surf, I said I didn't want to hop a turnstile.

"I have train money," I say.

"But hopping the stile is part of the fun." Mike won't let it go.

I look at Mike a long time. I feel played.

"You going under?" he asks Little Kevin.

"No doubt." He smiles. "But I never did before."

"Watch us," Mike says.

Mike ducks under the turnstile, and it shocks me that the MetroCard booth worker pays him no mind. His feet already disappear up the stairs.

I can't pay and let Mike and Little Kevin hop the turnstiles, so I go for it too.

I'm shocked again when I don't hear the MetroCard worker in the booth blast on the mic for me to pay my fare. Maybe it's too packed in here for her to notice short kids ducking under turnstiles.

I see Mike's kicks dip around a corner and I follow him. I wonder how Little Kevin is doing. Is he just standing there Stuck On Stupid the way I was when I first saw Mike not pay his fare way back in the day? I almost want to U-turn back to check on him.

Before I can, I know he ducks under the turnstile. I know because I hear a microphone shout, "Officers! Three boys didn't pay."

Officers?

I stop and look back, and two cops are chasing Kevin.

I don't stay to look. I keep walking toward the end of the platform, hoping Little Kevin can stay ahead of the cops and hop on the approaching train to book with us.

The train slows into the station, and I see Mike chilling at the end of the platform.

"COPS!" I tell him.

"What? Where?"

"Chasing Kevin!"

The train beeps, BOOP! BOOP! then the speakers on it say, "Stand clear of the closing doors," and we dive onto the back of the train.

As the train starts moving, I spot Little Kevin show up on the platform, heaving. I wish I could yell, "JUMP!" as we pass and I'd grab his hand midair and yank him onto the train's back with us. But that's some crazy movie stuff. There's no way he can climb on this train. And there's no way he can get on.

As the train zooms forward and we get closer, I see the two cops grab Little Kevin and shout at him.

My heart drops. I turn and yell at Mike, "THE COPS HAVE KEV!"

He can't hear me because of the outside sound, but Mike is grinning. His eyes look like I don't expect—happy. The cops've got Little Kevin, but Mike is just happy that he didn't get caught.

• • •

Mike elbows my shoulder, letting me know it's our stop. We get off in Manhattan and hustle onto the platform and jet up the stairs.

Outside, he grabs my forearm mad forcefully. He never touched me this hard. He whispers, "*You think the cops saw us?*"

I snatch my arm back. "Cops got Kev! And you just worried about you?!"

He looks around to see if anyone heard me. "Shut up."

"Don't tell me to shut up," I whisper, feeling my hands ball into fists. "You don't care that he's probably in some cop car heading to a police precinct now?"

He smirks. "I'm not worried. Because before today I told Kev if we ever got caught doing something, we never snitch on each other."

"Just because you told him don't? Puh-leez. Bruh, he could be snitching right now."

He shakes his head. "Nah. He ain't. I also told him if he drops dime, he'll catch a beatdown."

I look past Mike and wonder, *Catch a beatdown?* From who? Mike? From his friends?

I look at the names of streets and stores around us. "Why we get off in Manhattan? And here?"

"Brooklyn and Manhattan cops don't really talk. If BK cops radio each other, whatever. Manhattan cops probably won't hear it and won't check for us. But we need to forget China-town, the arcade, and everything. I'm not saying Kev snitched, but if he did, we can't go where he knows. We need to do new until this afternoon."

"Afternoon?! Bruh, I want to be back before that." I want to see my mom. I don't know why. I just really feel that right now.

"Around later in the afternoon is better. So if our fam knows, they had time to chill."

"Why you saying all this when you think Kev won't snitch?"

"We don't have to worry, trust me. But we can't be stupid."

Trust Mike? I don't trust him. I think of Little Kevin again.

This is too much too fast. First, cops. Next, who knows what's happening with Little Kevin? Now our parents might find out?

"Where you think Kev is?" I ask.

"Who cares?"

I look at Mike like I can't believe him, for real. Little Kevin stayed up under him like Mike was his big brother. Like Mike had Little Kevin's back. If only he could be here, hearing him right now.

"Yeah," I say, "but it's *our* fault he's in trouble."

He laughs under his breath. "It's not my fault. Who told him to follow us?"

I really can't believe Mike right now. And all of what's happening.

"Bust it, a Starbucks." He points across the street. "Let's go chill."

As he crosses the street to Starbucks without me, I look at the back of his head and wonder.

I wonder how he'd react if it was me who got caught by the cops.

People rush by me—all busy—in front of me, behind me. Some grown man almost knocks me over on his way somewhere. People are everywhere, but I feel alone in all this craziness. Craziness that I let myself get into for months. That I let myself get into right now. I feel like I can't talk to anyone about this stuff. I feel like I can't go anywhere to be safe and I hate it. I have so many feelings I don't know what to do. I stare at him disappearing into Starbucks. He's the only one who knows everything. He's the only one I *have* to trust. I hate it.

I rush and jaywalk to the Starbucks.

CHAPTER 29

It's almost two thirty when we're back on my block. I eye everyone, nervous someone knows.

Real fast, this really tall, thin sixth grader from another school rolls up on me and Mike on a scooter. I expect him to say he knows about us and Little Kevin. Instead, he kicks it with Mike about some nonsense. I relax a little.

But going in my building, Ava's reaction surprises us and makes me want to U-turn off my stoop and hop a train somewhere far off.

She puts her hand on her hip, cocking her head sideways, real salty. "*Wait* until you get upstairs."

Mike starts leaving. "Peace, Bryan. I gotta be home."

"Yeah!" Ava barks at his back. "Leave! Because *you* might be in trouble *too!*"

I watch him bounce, then I play dumb and smile at Ava. "What we in trouble for?"

She leaves, and I stand here Stuck On Stupid and dumb nervous. As she stomps upstairs, I stare at the stoop door. I should jet.

Ava yells down to me from the second floor. "Don't let me come get you. *Hurry up!*"

Dang! Dang-dang-dang-DANG! UGH!!!

• • •

Oh, dip. Pa is on the couch, cracking his knuckles over and over like he's about to throw someone a beatdown with his wild, bulging, googly eyes—all intense like he's kray. He stares at me like I'm the one about to catch the beatdown.

Little Kevin must've snitched. Now I'm about to catch wreck.

"Bryan." He grabs and holds up a torn open envelope from the couch. "What is this?!"

I look it up and down, trying to figure it out. I can't tell from across the room.

"Answer me! This says you missed school on days Ma says you were in school!"

Wait? What? This isn't about me train-surfing and Little Kevin getting caught by the cops? This is about me cutting school?

Pa stands and punches his thigh. "You go to school?! Or no?! Because if you cut school, I'll smack you!"

My eyes pop wide and bounce from Pa to Ava, then back to him.

Pa takes a step toward me, balling his free fist.

I imagine I'm Luke Cage. I brace myself for his smack. I imagine I won't feel anything.

Pa takes another step toward me. "Talk!"

I swallow hard. My mouth is mad dry and I'm so scared I can't get a word out.

127

"Tell him!" Ava says to me. My eyes meet hers. She doesn't want me to get smacked.

"I . . ." I look back at Pa. "I . . ."

"Joe!" Ma comes out of her bedroom. "Don't touch Bryan! You want me to call your parole officer?"

Pa's eyes slit.

He knows she *will* and that that call will send him back to jail.

He eyes me real angry as he leaves. Passing Ma, he tells her under his breath, "Keep babying him and watch! Watch what happens."

Ava folds her arms and nods like now *it's. About. To. Go. Down.*

She probably thinks what I do. Ma came to regulate.

"Ava, go to your room."

"What?" Ava's eyes go big. "Why?"

"Go." Ma is firm. "I need to talk to Bryan. Alone."

Whew! I am so lucky because Ma is all about talking.

She wants to know if the letter from school is true. She wants to know if I cut, who I cut with. She wants to know where I went when I wasn't in school. She tells me how sick to her stomach it makes her feel that she doesn't know where in the world I was when the whole time she thought I was safe in school. "Someone could've snatched you up. You could be dead."

I picture Mike. I remember him saying he told Little Kevin if he snitched, Little Kevin would catch a beatdown.

I look at Ma's eyes water up. I just want her to be happy and here I am doing this to her. She hunches over with her face in her hands and starts crying. Yo! She's sobbing hard for real.

Ava peeks out, sees Ma, and mouths to me, *I hate you.*

"I HATE YOU TOO!" I yell at Ava.

Ma's head snaps up. "Ava!"

Ava pokes her head back in her door and slams it.

"Mike." I whisper that to Ma without realizing it. Then I stop myself. I can't hit her with everything. The way she is right now, she'd have a heart attack and die.

"Mike?" Ma wipes tears from her cheeks.

I nod. "We cut those times. Just to chill on the roof."

"Our roof?"

"Yeah," I lie. Ma knows folks all over our projects because of her job. If people have complained of kids throwing rocks at cars from roofs and I tell Ma we've been on mad roofs, she'll know it was Mike and that I was with him.

Ma takes a deep breath in. "You and him doing anything? Anything I should know about?"

I shake my head. "Like?"

"Smoking. Drinking. Anything a middle-school boy shouldn't do?"

"Nah, never," I tell her and that part's the truth. Then everything else we've done flashes in my mind. Hopping train-station turnstiles. The different neighborhoods. Train-surfing and . . .

"We just chill upstairs and draw," I say, "and read comics. That's it. Because school is dead."

"What?"

"Corny. School is corny sometimes."

129

Ma believes me, relaxing back into the couch and putting one hand on her head. I feel like she's about to say I can't see Mike no more. I feel like she's about to list mad punishments and ground me for forever. But she bites her lip and says, "You and him are too young to do this. It has to stop, okay? And I need to talk to him."

I nod.

"But I don't want you talking to him. Not until I do and figure things out. And you're grounded. You're not going out today or tomorrow. And your father and I will figure out more punishment for you."

• • •

The rest of the night I feel four things.

First, I can't believe the school sent Ma a letter about me cutting.

Next, whoa! I got busted for only that?!

Third, Pa almost smacked me into tomorrow.

Fourth, I do everything half expecting cops or someone to knock on the door and—*boom*—everything with Little Kevin gets found out.

Eight o'clock passes. Nine. Ten. Then it's time for bed.

Lying in bed, I stare at the ceiling. I can't sleep. I didn't hear nothing about Little Kevin tonight. But tomorrow?

CHAPTER 30

Two days later on Monday morning, Pa and Ava eye me real mean during breakfast.

Ma walks me to school like I'm in kindergarten again.

It's mad embarrassing. I'm the only middle-school kid walking up our school's block with a parent. Kids stop talking as we get close, and they stare and say stuff under their breaths about me as we walk by. I feel like such a herb. Ma doesn't care. She wants to talk with my teachers and make me apologize for my cutting. She wants to get the whole scoop about how many days and assignments I've missed. She wants to do another thing: She wants to see Mike.

I get to him before she does because I know where he chills in the morning and she doesn't.

"I need to pee," I tell her after she signs in at the security desk near the main office.

"Hurry."

And just like that, I stroll chill-like around the corner toward the bathroom, then jet past it down the stairs—two steps at a time—huff past the gym, tackle open the doors, and spot Mike where he hangs with other seventh graders and a few sixth graders in the courtyard. I race to him. As I get close, dudes he's with tap him and say stuff like, "Yo, your brother," and point, "Ayo, your bruh." Before, I loved hearing that. Now? Not so much.

I get to him. "Whattup," I nod at everyone, then look dead at him. "Come talk."

He leaves the dudes he's with. "'Sup?"

I wipe sweat off my forehead and speak fast. "Ma's here. School sent a letter listing days I been absent. You got one?"

"I get them before my moms and I tear them up."

"Dummy. Why you didn't say school sends those home? I could've been on the lookout."

"Forgot."

"Ugh! How could you forget that! Now Ma is here to find out stuff with my teachers. And she wants to see you before she leaves."

"Me?! Dang, you snitch! Why me?!"

I look at him like he must be dumb. My mom is *really* here and *really* about to see *all* my teachers. I'm the one in deep doo-doo and here he is *again* only worried about himself. For real, *for real*?

"I'm not a snitch," I say. "But she knew I had to be with you. So I just told her me and you cut and stayed on my roof, drawing and reading comics."

"Ugh."

"I need to be out. Ma's about to go to my first class with me. Remember, we just cut to be on one roof, my roof."

I turn to go and he grabs my forearm. "What if your moms tells mine? They talk. She will."

"Then handle that. It's better than them knowing *everything* we've got into. And where's Little Kevin at, anyway? He usually runs around here. You heard what ended up happening with him and the cops?"

Mike shakes his head.

"A'ight. I'm out."

I jet.

• • •

Ms. Whitman goes all the way in, even telling Ma all about the notes I gave her written in Ma's handwriting. "You mean, they weren't from you?"

Ma side-eyes me like she could backhand-smack me out my chair and send me crashing out the window.

When Ma's meeting with her is over, Ma walks me out of class.

Her face turns seriouser than serious. "Where'd you learn to write like me?"

I wish I could say Mike. "I . . . I . . . me."

I look at my kicks. I feel grimy. Me and Ma used to have the bomb relationship. I used to be able to tell her anything. Now, I lie to her left and right for Mike, who probably gives two craps about me.

Ma says the worst. "I should let your father punish you. Leave you with him in the house and let him do whatever. Because I don't know . . ."

What?! She wouldn't! Will she?

Just the thought makes me nervously swallow, and my stomach and legs tremble.

One time when I was nine, I slipped and said a curse in front of him and he took me home and OD'd on me. He said, "You wanna talk like a man? I'll smack your face like a man!" I was so happy Ma was home and heard him. She ran into the living room and stopped him.

The thought right now of her leaving me alone with him fires me up all jumpy, like when Pop Rocks are on my tongue.

And the rest of Ma's school visit gets worse. She collects so many assignments I missed—plus lots of extra ones for punishment—that before she leaves me there, she hands me a stack of papers so high that they're almost too heavy for me to hold up.

"You're doing all of this."

What?! I'll be writing until my hand cramps.

"After school, you come straight to my job. No Mike. You have all of this to do and extra assignments that I'm making for you."

"Are you letting Pa punish me?" I ask.

Ma turns and walks to a stairwell door.

I stand there, my thoughts now popping like Pop Rocks in an oily frying pan. She didn't answer. Does that mean yes?

Right before the door closes, she side-eyes me. "That depends on how fast you make up that missed work. *And* how well you do on them. Mike is in seven-three-oh-two, right?"

I nod.

Yo! After school, I'm booking to her job like the Flash. And

I'm gonna do every assignment perfect. No matter how long it takes. She *is not* leaving me alone with Pa.

• • •

After Ma leaves, I spend the day feeling three things. First, too embarrassed to make eye contact with my teachers. Next, scared from yesterday—that any minute a cop or someone would show up with Little Kevin and it would be a wrap for me and Mike. Third, worried—anytime outside of class when crowds of kids are around, I scan for Little Kevin. Dude is nowhere.

The whole day passes with me feeling those three ways on loop, and soon school is over.

At dismissal, me and Mike end up in the same loud crowd rolling down the stairwell that leads out the side of our school. I spot him way ahead at the bottom of the steps, and I U-turn real fast before anyone can tell him, "Yo, your brother," or something.

I can't see him because I'm not risking more punishment by being seen with him, but I'm fiending to know how Ma's convo with him went.

I go against the crowd back up to the second floor and exit on the opposite side of the building.

• • •

At Ma's work, nobody knows the trouble I'm in.

The janitor—Mr. Roberts—talks to me like he usually does like I'm going to be president of the United States someday. He even says stuff like that. "Hey, Mr. Man." He soft-punches my arm as I come out of the bathroom. "When you running for mayor?"

I shrug.

The two secretaries—Ms. Torres and Ms. Betancourt—who treat me like I'm the coolest kid on earth start talking to me from their desks. "Is it me? Or is Bryan taller than the last time we saw him?" Ms. Torres winks at Ms. Betancourt, then says—because she knows I'm a sixth grader but is just playing—"What? Bryan, you're an eighth grader now?"

Ma's coworkers have me feeling up from all their compliments.

I look at Ma, who stands at her desk and eyes me like she did before in school. She's still pissed. I don't know why, but I flip from feeling up to feeling like I don't deserve props from her coworkers. I look back at Ms. Torres and Ms. Betancourt and fake a smile and keep it moving.

In my office, I pull the first handout on top of the dumb high stack of assignments I need to make up. It's math and I wish I hadn't cut because I don't understand this.

When Big Will showed me that TV show *Heroes* on his phone, there was this kid who looks like me who has a power I wish I could flex right now. Micah. Micah is mad smart and puts his hands on computers and downloads information. When he touches any electronics, they talk to him. Man, if I was Micah, I'd go swipe my hand over one of these computers in here and know how to do all these makeup assignments. I flick through the rest of the stacks. *Ugh!* I don't understand most of this. I finally find a literacy assignment I can do, easy. I slide it out and get to work.

"Did you double-check it?"

Ma doesn't even look at the literacy assignment in her hand that I just knocked out.

The truth is no. I didn't double-check it.

She eyes me like, *Don't lie,* and I'm already in trouble for lying so I take it back. "I'll double-check it."

"Good."

Ma calls me back as I walk away. "I spoke to Mike."

"And?"

"You don't need to see him for a while."

I want to know about her conversation with him—not that I can't hang with him. I stand there, waiting for that info.

"That's it. Go do your work."

"For how long?" I ask. "How long am I not supposed to hang with him."

"Until I say. That means at school too. Don't let me and Pa find out you are."

There she goes again: Pa. She already threatened to leave me alone with Pa, so she doesn't have to tell me twice to stay away from Mike. Done.

CHAPTER 31

"You avoiding me."

Hearing Mike's voice, I wish I could teleport like Night-crawler from the *X-Men* so fast and disappear from here and pop up in my next class so I don't have to turn around and tell him some lie about why I've dodged him all day like *Ms. Pac-Man* shakes ghosts.

I turn around, fake a smile, and put my fist out for a fist-bump. "Nah, bruh, I just been on my school grind. Ma wants me making up *everything* I missed."

"She told me that junk too. Your ma is OD corny, thinking I'm listening to her. Psst. Puhleez. And she said me and you shouldn't chill until she says so. Sometimes, she can be . . . Any-way, change subjects. We chilling after school?"

Nobody needs to tell me my eyes are wild googly like I want to flip right now. I feel them. First, I don't like *nobody* dissing Ma. Next, he has nerve. After all he did, he thinks my moms is in the wrong?

"What you looking at me like that for?" he asks.

"Why you cutting on my moms?"

"Psst"—he sucks his teeth—"you know she's corny some-times. Stop playing."

Little Kevin pops up in my mind. Since Mike's here, I want to know what's the dilly with Little Kevin. "What's up with Kev?"

He looks off like Little Kevin is the last thing he wants to discuss right now. "It's all good." He licks his lips and smirks. "Nothing is happening."

"How nothing?"

He slowly turns and stares at me like I'm some joke. "Noth-ing, *like nothing.*"

"The cops snatched him and nothing happened?"

"Yeah. He didn't drop our names and he's not in big trouble."

"So what little trouble is he in?"

"Cops do something sometimes when a kid is too young to be charged. They put a report on what the kid did in a file and keep it until he's eighteen. That's what Kev told me they did. They called his moms to the precinct and explained if cops catch Kev doing wrong again before he's eighteen, then he's in big trouble. But if he doesn't do anything, they'll throw out his file when he turns eighteen. No crime, no time."

I feel so happy for Little Kevin. I also feel relieved me and Mike won't catch heat.

He interrupts my thoughts. "Forget Kev. So, we chilling at dismissal or you being a nerd?"

I look at him like he can't be serious. He's saying forget Kev, then herbing me and calling me a nerd?

I start walking away. "I guess I'll be a nerd."

Mike yells at my back as kids move in between us. "Why you gotta be wack, for real?"

I breathe in deep to cool down.

• • •

In school that first week of avoiding Mike, he side-eyes and sucks his teeth at me more and more from far off.

And something else happens at home. Pa's voice comes from behind me as I'm getting something off the bottom shelf of our fridge. "Bryan, you've been talking to Mike?"

"No."

His eyes study my whole face for one sign that I'm lying. "Good."

That catches me off guard. "How come?"

"I was outside Hector's bodega," Pa says, "and Mike started walking toward me like nothing ever happened. It took a lot for me not to yell at him for getting you in trouble. So, I just told him I'm disappointed in him and he better realize I'm good to him as long as he's good to you."

The fact that Pa did that makes me know three things: First, Pa has my back. Next, Pa isn't talking to Mike, which must make Mike feel like crap. Third, no wonder Mike has been sucking his teeth at me more and more—he's probably extra tight that he's been cut off from my family so hard.

I know this is true because a week of Mike side-eyeing me turns into another week of him tapping whoever is next to him to say something nasty, probably something about me.

I'm happy to go to Ma's job in the afternoons. It's peaceful. It feels more like how after-school used to be. And I feel more like the old me there.

Anytime I need a break from doing schoolwork, I draw or read comics. I don't know where Ma is getting the loot, but she bought me seven new ones. And I don't know who's telling her what to pick, but she picked the best ones. Wavy art. *Black Panther* and *Batman* and ones that're movies or about to be movies.

I won't say I love spending *every* afternoon at Ma's job in my office, because I'm still doing makeup work and it's not as exciting as everything me and Mike chased. But, still, it's sort of dip.

CHAPTER 32

All the weeks of me not kicking it with Mike means lots of weeks of me kicking it more with Big Will.

We talk *Ms. Pac-Man*. He shows me more *Heroes* episodes on his phone outside at dismissal. Once, I point at Big Will's screen. "You got Netflix?"

"Yeah." He nods as he keeps watching *Heroes*.

I ask, "You heard of Luke Cage?"

"Nah. Who that?"

"A superhero you might like. Search him on Netflix."

"You have Netflix too?" he asks. "You saw his show?"

"Nah. I know him from comics. But I heard he has a show. Let's see."

Big Will types fast, finds, and plays season one, episode one, and scrolls fast-forward to this whoa action scene!

I already knew Luke Cage could pass for somebody in my family or Mike's because he's drawn Black in comics. He's darker than me and Mike but looks like my cousin Diego and Mike's oldest brother Randy. But Luke Cage is way more in shape. He could be a WWE wrestler. Now seeing Luke Cage as a real person and not drawn is straight whoa. The actor who plays Luke looks *pissed* right now. Luke Cage puts on his black hoodie over his baldie, walks to a parked black SUV Jeep, and *rips* the door off with his bare hands! He carries it like a shield and stomps up the stoop of a projects building that matches mine, uses the SUV car door to smash down the front-stoop door, walks in, and it gets so crazy that me and Big Will look at each other like *YOOOOO*, then back at the screen!

Me and Big Will grip his cell phone tighter and lean in. The action gets crazier and crazier. When Big Will's alarm on his phone goes off, we're mad.

"Ugh!" he says. "I have to go! My moms is waiting for me. Baseball practice."

• • •

For the next three weeks, it's like this with Big Will.

Three weeks of chillness after school on our school's corner. Us watching *Heroes* and *Luke Cage* on Netflix on his phone.

Three weeks of no drama.

I like that Big Will is different and never acts like he has to prove anything.

Most guys who don't know each other do this stare-off thing and eye each other like *What you looking at?* It's a way to show everyone you're not soft. Tough guys respect tough guys and mostly let each other pass.

I've never tried staring hard back at guys because I have Pa. Nobody wants beef with him so they don't beef with me.

Big Will doesn't do the stare-off thing either. I figured at first it's because of his size. But then one afternoon I learned he has a different attitude.

We just left school and walk through a corner thick with older guys from our school. It's like a video game steering between each one without bumping into anybody. And we do it until—*thump*—Big Will's shoulder accidentally knocks hard against the shoulder of this eighth-grade boy whose name I don't know. From the looks of the older guy, he's the last boy you want to bump into. He's as big as Big Will, and his face says "drama" and he doesn't mind if he's in it. His clothes and sneakers say swag and he's ready to fight if someone messes that up.

As I think, *Oh, dip, we're about to be in a fight,* I notice Big Will reacts completely different than most guys would. As the eighth-grade boy says "Yo" and steps toward Big Will, Big Will steps back all calm and puts his open hands up in an apologizing way, and says, "My bad."

The eighth grader's face slowly relaxes, and he turns to see if his friends heard Big Will. They nod and he looks back at us and nods like we're free to go.

Okay, before I thought it was Big Will's size that made dudes back down, but I know this isn't the reason now.

As we leave the corner, I think hard about what Big Will just did. "That was cool," I tell him. "How you calmed that kid down. I thought he was going to try to fight you."

"He *was* getting hyped," Big Will says. "Which is why I tried to cool him down. Bryan, if someone wants to think they're

144

tougher than me, I let them. I just say 'My bad' and that usually makes them feel boss. 'My bad' usually relaxes someone who is tight and starting to hype themselves up."

"It works all the time?"

"Yeah." He thinks for a few seconds. "But I guess if someone is really looking for trouble, no amount of 'My bads' will work."

"But it always worked for you?"

"Yeah."

My bad, I think. I like that.

Big Will and I walk to the back of our projects, then out of them to the piers and sit on a bench that faces the Statue of Liberty. It's a new part of this piers I've never been to. From here, the Statue of Liberty feels just a few blocks from us, like if sidewalks magically rose out of the river's waves, we could walk to the Statue of Liberty real quick.

We sit there quiet for the longest time, staring at stuff. The waves go up and down, seagulls in the air not too far from us do that hang-glidey thing, and I inhale deep, breathing in the fresh air. It has a saltiness in it like we're at the beach. The sun is starting to set, and the sky is full of colors and looks like a painting.

The feeling I have now is the feeling I had in Starbucks. It's the feeling I have with Ma at the Promenade. Just sitting, just chilling, and far away from our projects' drama.

Just when I'm thinking this whole scene is mad peaceful, Big Will says, "Someday I'm living in a place where I can watch the sun set like this every day. From my window."

I look at Will and say, "For real?"

He shrugs. "I hope so. This is my thing: peace, quiet, no drama. Y'feel me?"

I smile, but more at myself because I realize three things. First, Will is reading my mind and says what I really want life to be like. Second, I smile because I realize that he's the type of friend I want more of. The third reason I smile is I just now notice Melanie from school is five benches away talking with three of her girlfriends from school. As I think it's cool that she likes it back here too, she looks over and waves for me and Big Will to come over.

I elbow Big Will and we join them.

One of Melanie's friends looks at Big Will like he's familiar. "You're ..."

He laughs. "Big Will."

"Big Will?" She smiles this not-mean smile and I know because some girls and boys are about that drama and smirk, giggle, and laugh at people's nicknames. Not her. Not now. She reaches for his hand to shake. "Big Will because ... ?"

Big Will shakes her hand and jokes, "Because I'm so tiny?"

They smile some more.

"I'm Christina." She makes room for him. "Sit."

Big Will and her start talking and soon I hear them chatting about *Ms. Pac-Man*.

Sasha, Melanie's other friend, leans over into his conversation and tells Big Will, "You said *Ms. Pac-Man*? That's my game too."

He points to me. "Then Bryan's the one you should play.

He's the man. I can't play like him. He posts the new high score every time."

It feels good hearing him say I'm the man and I realize something else is different about Big Will. He's putting me up. If it was Mike, Mike would be putting me down.

I jump in the conversation and start sharing my *Ms. Pac-Man* strategies and I realize something else when Melanie, Christina, Sasha, say "Yup, yup" and "True" and "Us too" to me when I say, "*Ms. Pac-Man* gives me that same rush I get when I play handball."

Melanie and her girls are like homeboys and they're different than I expected. I knew Melanie was a nice person, but she and her friends are into handball? And *Ms. Pac-Man*? And Big Will gets along with her friends like they've known each other forever?

"This your first time coming to the pier?" I ask Melanie out of the blue.

She makes a face like back here is heaven. "What? We're here all the time. If we're not playing *Ms. Pac-Man*, *Galaga*, and other old-school video games in that arcade on Sullivan Street."

"What?!" me and Big Will say at the same time.

I ask, "There's another arcade back here?"

"Yeah," Melanie said. "But it's run by a family, so they keep it private because they don't want just anyone in there. You both should come there with us."

Yo. Melanie's timing and her saying that is lit. First, I *just*

147

was wishing I had more friends like Big Will, and now here she and her friends are acting so chill and trying to make that happen. I'm amped.

• • •

So yeah, the three weeks hanging with just Will was real good. It was three weeks of me feeling closer to where I should be and closer to who I am.

But it was also three weeks of me seeing Mike look more and more heated anytime his eyes are on me. Whenever I see him, bruh's face looks like a boiling pot of water about to bubble over.

I should've known something was coming. If I were Batman, I would've since he thinks like ten steps ahead.

CHAPTER 33

Wednesday after dismissal, me and Big Will chill on a corner of our school and compare the powers of Nightcrawler from the *X-Men* to Hiro from *Heroes*.

"Hiro is better," Big Will says, "because, bust it, he does more than teleport. He time-travels and can stop ti—"

Mike interrupts.

Well, not Mike. Dennis and Christian do. Mike and Little Kevin stand behind them. They're two sixth graders I never speak to. They're both my size. I look at Little Kevin and nod whattup at him. He stares at me with no expression like we have no history. I can't believe him. After Mike got him arrested, he still follows him.

"Bryan," Dennis tells me, "we gonna play handball. Come."

Honestly, Dennis pays me no mind in school, so I wonder why he's up on me like we tight.

I look at Mike, but I answer Dennis. "Can't."

Now it's Christian talking. "Why?"

What's up with these guys who treat me like a hole in the wall, asking me to hang out and then why I can't?

"Ask Mike," I say. "He knows."

Dennis turns to Christian. "Son, you gonna let him catch that tone with you?"

What?! I think. *I said "Ask Mike" with no tone.*

All I can see is Dennis's face. Then Christian's. Their expressions match that villain Killmonger who fights Black Panther and every evil comic villain who fights anyone. Their faces match Mike's the times I've caught him eyeing me funny.

Dennis and Christian came to throw hands.

Then I hear it: "Your moms."

I swing around quick. "What?!"

Dennis says, "I *said*, 'Run home to your pops and moms.'"

I look at him, then at Mike. Now his face matches theirs.

"Yo." I step toward them without knowing it. "Keep my moms *and* pops out your mouths."

I notice Dennis's face change. His bravery is gone. Mike must've put him up to this. Maybe told him I'm soft. But now Dennis doesn't want a fight.

Christian does. "Or what?" Christian steps toward me. "Your moms. Now what?"

I want to punch his face. Nah, I want to punch *through* it. My heart races. But I'm not scared. I'm not.

I step toward him. "Say 'my moms' to my face."

Then I feel it. These arms python-squeeze around me, pinning mine to my sides. *Yo!* Who is straight lifting me up off the floor and back to school?!

I turn my head to see who has me in this tight grip. It's Big Will.

"Bring him back!" Christian yells at Big Will.

I yell at Big Will too while trying to break free. "Let me go!"

Big Will puts me down but doesn't let go. He's using his big body to block Christian in case he tries running up on me.

Yo! Big Will definitely has more muscles as well as more facial hair than any sixth grader I know. He's mad strong and I bet he could handle them alone.

Now more kids are here, and a little crowd is in between Christian and me. I notice Mike looks at me and he tries to hide his surprise at my reaction. He doesn't look evil anymore. He looks like those times he's studied my reaction like he was collecting info for a later day. I look at Little Kevin. He's all wide-eyed like watching this fight almost pop off was the hotness.

Mike taps Christian and motions for him to leave. Mike says something to him as they walk away, and I think I can tell what it is but I'm not sure because we're a little far but not that far. "Chill. Bryan can't fight. He never been in one."

What the—? Did he just tell Christian something I told him back in the day? He's such a—

Big Will spins me around to him, while keeping his hands gripped on both of my shoulders. "You look like you almost Hulked out over there."

"He said my moms."

"Yeah, well, you went psycho, bruh. I was scared for him." Big Will wraps his arm around me. "Let's go this way," he says, leading me the opposite way from Mike and them. I can't tell if he has his arm around me to seize me up in another python grip in case I try running after Christian to fight or if he has his arm around me brother-like.

151

Big Will laughs and says it again: "You went psycho, kid. I was really scared for him."

I don't speak. Because I don't know what I would've done. I've never had a fight. I was just so mad. My punches probably are no better than when Ava teased me about them—she probably still punches harder than me.

"You have a temper," Big Will says, interrupting my thoughts.

You have a temper. That is what Pa says.

Look at his eyes. That's what Mike said about the fighters who win.

Could I have really hurt Christian?

Big Will keeps on. "And your whole everything just flipped. Your eyes, your body. Everything about you was just no joke. You looked hard-core, like Luke Cage, for real."

CHAPTER 34

Ma's eyes follow me and Big Will as we walk into her job.

Her eyes follow me as I go to my office.

"Sit wherever," I tell Big Will as I unzip my backpack, move to my file cabinet, and look for Ma. Her eyes still follow me.

Then she comes over. "What's up?"

She doesn't ask who is Big Will, even though she's never met him. She's not asking me "What's up?" to know about my day. She's asks like she *knows* something just happened with me.

She and Big Will look for my reaction.

I give her my back so she doesn't see my face, and I pretend to put the homework handouts in my hands in order.

"Bryan, turn around."

I do and force a fake smile. "Uh-huh?"

Ma squints like my left eye has a paragraph in it and my right eye has a paragraph, and she reads them.

"Why do your eyes look like that?"

"Like what?"

"Like—"

She doesn't say it probably because Big Will is in here and Ma doesn't like putting our family business out on the street. But I bet she was about to say *Like Pa's*. Hyped, kray eyes.

On the tip of my tongue is how Mike just set me up to fight. I want to tell her so bad. I hold back telling her though. I'm not a snitch. And I don't want her telling Pa or Ava because that'll get them thinking I'm soft and that I can't handle Mike on my own. Plus, I don't even think this will happen again. I think he was just hurt that I stopped hanging with him.

"So?" Ma interrupts my thoughts. "What just happened?"

"This," I lie and hold up my stack of assignments. "It's just OD hard to catch up on so much! It's *too* much. I don't feel like I'll ever catch up!"

Ma cocks her head to one side, trying to figure out if this is what's up with me.

Big Will eyes me, shocked like, *Oh, you not telling her.*

"Well, it's your fault," Ma tells me. "Take breaks and draw or read comics like you do. But you got yourself into this mess. Who is your friend?"

"This is Will. He's in sixth grade in my school. Can he stay and do homework with me? He's on the honor roll."

Ma smiles friendly at him while analyzing to see if he's a "good kid."

"Who's your family?"

"Mr. and Mrs. Ramos are my mom and dad."

My moms nods like she knows them. "You're Julianne and Juan's son?"

Big Will nods.

Wow. Ma knows everyone.

She reaches for a handshake. "Hi, I'm Bryan's mom. I've met your parents through my work here before."

He reaches for Ma's hand. "Nice to meet you, miss."

They shake hands and she leaves.

I pull a stack of comics out of my desk and hand them to Big Will.

He's too hyped and goes all the way in to reading them.

I go to my file cabinet.

I hid something in there that I never told anyone. Back when I did, I put it in a big yellow envelope from Ma's job, then taped it shut.

I find the envelope, then eye Big Will. He's lost in the sauce with those comics.

I look back at the envelope in the drawer and break the tape, pull what I hid in it out, and study it.

It's a drawing Mike drew and gave me when we first became tight. It's one of his best.

He drew me as Batman but with my face and my Afro hair. That's because when he asked me which hero I'd be, I told him Batman because he's the world's smartest detective or I'd be Black Panther since he's as smart as Batman. They figure out stuff mad fast and know what's happening ten steps ahead. In his drawing, he drew himself next to me as Luke Cage. Back then, he chose him because "Nothing hurts him."

I look and look at Luke Cage.

Right now, I wish again I were Luke Cage.

Mike isn't Luke Cage. Luke's good. The way Mike acted

back at school, he should be the Joker, Batman's main enemy, or Killmonger, Black Panther's main enemy. That's how Mike is acting.

I hope he stops.

I look at the lower right-hand corner of the drawing at the way he signed "Mike" like he is a for real artist, and it makes me miss him just a little.

I slide the drawing back in its yellow envelope then shut the file cabinet drawer.

I turn and Big Will is still oblivious and is SOS happy reading my comics.

I think about how different me and Big Will's friendship is from me and Mike's. It's just chill and fun and there's no drama. He gets amped about *Ms. Pac-Man* the way I do. He wants me to get high scores in that game and doesn't ever flash me weird, jealous looks. And he geeks out, for real. Not like Mike, who pretends to Ma that he likes school but is more hypnotized by dudes pushing fat whips with shiny dip rims.

I look out at Ma and everyone in her job and there's that peacefulness again. No phones ring, just pencils and pens scratchy-scribble on papers, and there's no drama anywhere. Right now, I listen to the sounds of my pretend-office and only hear Big Will's breathing as he's all into his comic. This is what I'm talking about: this comfortable feeling of chillness. A chillness I thought I could have with Mike but now I just don't know.

CHAPTER 35

The next day, Mike strolls into Ma's job as I knock out my homework alone in my office.

As he heads to Ma's desk I think, *Oooh. He's about to get it! He knows Ma is mad at him.*

From the way he bows his head as he speaks and how he holds his hands out, though, it looks like he's apologizing. And it looks like it's working on Ma. She waves for him to sit.

I'm mad curious. Why is here? What're they talking about?

I'm Stuck On Stupid and can't take my eyes off them for the fifteen minutes they talk.

Ma and him stand, and my eyes pop when *they hug*. Then, she rests her hand on Mike's back and walks him in my direction.

Wait! What's happening?

Ma and him arrive. "Mike wants to tell you something."

I fold my arms because all I want to hear is sorry. Bruh got me in trouble and set me up to fight. And all this time without him, I've had no drama.

"I'll leave you two to talk." Ma goes back to her desk.

157

Mike slowly looks up at me. His face his straight ashamed for real. "Bryan, I was foul." He nods at an empty chair. "Can I sit?"

I nod yes.

He gets right into it. He's sorry about suggesting I cut school. He's sorry about the almost fight with Dennis and Christian. The more he apologizes, the more ashamed he looks.

"You . . . ," he says, "you like my brother. For real. I didn't want you in trouble like this." He keeps on apologizing about name-calling me, Dennis and Christian, and it really doesn't matter what he says because of what I feel. I'm OD glad that he's acting different and wants things different between us.

But a part of me is confused. "What made you come in here?"

"My moms."

Really? I never knew his mom thought twice about me and his friendship. "Why?"

"She said you a real friend and I shouldn't crap on real friends. So?"

"So what?"

"Want to see some new comics I got?"

"What you tell my moms just now?"

Mike looks at her as she handles a work phone call. "Not the whole. Just I'm sorry I hung with you on the roofs when I could've been a better friend and made us go to school."

I look at my moms now. "You didn't tell her the whole be-cause—"

Mike jumps in. "Because she doesn't need to know the

whole. Just that I'm sorry and won't be getting you in trouble again."

"You pushed Dennis and Christian to beef with me."

"And I'm a herb for it. That won't happen again and I won't put you in drama, *ever* again. I'm telling you—that's my word."

"Word."

We fist-bump.

He pulls his new comics out his backpack and we flip through them.

It sort of feels like old times.

CHAPTER 36

Ma won't let me be over at Mike's and she won't let him chill in our apartment. She says something about "take it slow." But she lets us hang outside and in her job.

When we break from playing basketball on the court that Carmelo Anthony donated to our projects, me and him chill on a bench and he sees me OD reread his newest Luke Cage comic for the fourth, fifth time.

"Take that," Mike says.

I slap it shut and try handing it to him. I don't want his hand-out. It makes me feel like a broke bum beggar. "Nah."

"That's yours." He pushes the comic back at me. "You hit me off with stuff all week. Let me pay you back with that."

"Nah."

He pushes the comic back at me, again. "I'm *telling* you—that's *yours.*"

I zip it in my backpack. For the rest of the day, I expect him to ask for it back. He doesn't.

Heads on the street flex back to treating us like we close brothers, even Dennis and Christian, who Mike yeasted up to fight me. They even apologize to me. But I see it in Christian's eyes—he's not sorry. If me and Mike fell off again, he'd fight me again.

Lately, I've been hanging some with Big Will too, but in these moments I wonder why I don't just hang all the time with him. Because he's cool. Plus, he's good backup.

When Ma lets Mike back into our apartment, first he acts like nothing bad ever happened between us.

Then a few days later he starts acting a little too comfortable in my bedroom—kicking his sneakers at my wall and flinging his coat on my floor. He eyes me like he wants to see if I ask him to pick his stuff up.

I ignore him and flip through my *Black Panther* comic. "When we weren't hanging," I say, "I found out that Black Panther trained and has reflexes better than a real wildcat or panther."

Too quick, Mike sucks his teeth. "That's garbage information."

Little by little, day after day, it feels like Mike's real attitude and anger boil more and more to the surface. It's like everything he does I could list in a game of I Get Annoyed When.

Soon, he starts strolling in my apartment like whatever-whatever hostile. Like all he sees when he sees me is his memory of everything that upset him about past garbage. He rocks the same cocky face and cocky body language I've seen on him before but now he's *extra*. I wonder why he is acting this way when I don't act ill with him.

One afternoon Mike comes into our apartment and puts his feet up on the couch, acting like he owns the place.

I point at his kicks. "Ma doesn't like sneakers on the couch."

He doesn't move.

"Can you please," I repeat softly and point at his kicks again, "move your feet?"

He snaps, "Calm down!" then beasts louder. "It ain't that serious!"

He slowly moves his feet.

I try to be nice and make conversation. "Where you just came from?"

He stands, brushes by me, knocking his shoulder into mine, hard. "Hanging. With Christian."

He grabs this mini Nerf basketball that Ma just bought me. Anything Ma buys me is special to me.

Mike tosses it from one hand to his other. Immediately, I don't want him touching it.

"So, you best friends with Big Will now?" He looks and sounds extra salty, like the way he was when he came into Ma's job and saw me having fun with that kid Kamau.

"Why is me and Big Will being cool a problem?" I say. "I don't care if you cool with Christian. And can you put my ball down?"

He flings it on Ma's dinner table like *whoa*, knocking a plastic cup of pens over. Without looking at me, he says some gibberish I can't understand ending with "And you made your dad not talk to me for weeks."

He swings around and the look on his face! Yo! He growls the next thing real clear. "So why you keep acting soft, hanging out with nerds?"

I look at that spilled cup. I hear his word *soft*. My heart races. I nervous-chuckle. "Don't call me soft."

"But you *are*. That's probably the only reason you hang with stupid Big Will. Because his size and he can protect your soft butt."

My mouth gets dry. I think about Big Will's advice: Say "My bad" because it usually relaxes someone who is tight. I go open my apartment door. "My bad, Mike. You right. About everything. But you should bounce. Maybe come back when everyone is here and we can talk then."

Mike ignores me and goes to the table and picks up a new comic Ma just got me as reward for finally catching up with my makeup assignments. "This is nice."

He flings it on the floor.

I'm tight and the anger in me is building, so I breathe in deep the way Ma taught me to not lose control. I hold the door open wider. "You need to be out now."

He bops up to me so close that I smell the mint gum he chews. He slams the apartment door shut and snarls in my face. "Make me."

What the—? He's acting like he's ready to beast on me.

I walk farther away. "You playing?"

He laughs. "No! I'm *not*."

He picks up the Nerf basketball he just tossed on my dinner table. "It's mine now."

"Put it back."

He holds the Nerf ball out. "Take it."

When I try grabbing for it, he snatches it away.

Whoa. What's wrong with him? I'm done playing his stupid game. I turn to walk away when—

Smack.

Yo. He just *soft-smacked* me.

His face grins all the way max like the Joker's. "Do something."

My warning comes out as a whisper. "*Get out.*"

He snarls, all cocky, "Or? What?"

He smacks me again and then shoves me hard, and I start feeling those feelings in my gut that I felt when Christian hopped in my face to fight.

He bumps his nose against mine, saying, "Oh, that's right. You never been in a fight, so you aren't going to do anything. Right? *Punk?*"

Every explosion I've ever stopped from exploding in me when he did something grimy to me explodes now and I let my temper go.

Real fast, I wrap my arms around his waist, lift, and body-slam him.

He scrambles back onto his feet and punches for my head. I duck and let my fists fly.

And I connect.

My blows tag his nose, stomach, arms, and I keep swinging until I back him into a corner. I imagine I'm the Flash and start throwing faster and faster punches.

He mainly blocks, then weak-swings twice—punching the top of my head, then missing.

I uppercut him. "You Luke Cage? Huh?"

I punch him again near his ear. "You Luke Cage, BRUH?!"

I imagine I'm Luke Cage when he punched one guy through the ceiling. I hit Mike harder. "Nah Mike! *I'M* LUKE CAGE!"

I puff up. I feel unbreakable like Luke Cage. I yell, "YOU THINK I'M SOFT?! HIT ME!"

He punches my jaw and goes to swing on me again, but I dodge him. I knee him in his groin hard, and he drops. I manage to mount him and use my knees to pin down his arms. "YOU AIN'T NO HERO! YOU A BAD GUY! AND YOU GONNA STOP BULLYING ME!"

Right then, my sister busts through the apartment door and drags me off him. I let her.

"Stop!" She shoves me against the wall.

"He hit me first!" I stutter. "He . . . he came in here and he . . . he started smacking me and disrespecting Ma!"

Ava sticks her finger in my face. "You. Stay. HERE!"

I do.

She goes to Mike, who's crying on the floor, and she checks his face.

He jumps up, yelling at me, "YOU GONNA CATCH A BEAT-DOWN!"

He runs at me and I put my fists up, but he runs by me to leave our apartment.

As the door opens, I run to follow and give him a last kick in his butt, but Ava grabs me.

"Stop!" She holds my arms tight. "You hurt him enough!"

The hyped look on Ava's face doesn't even match how hyped I feel.

I'm so up I feel like I just mashed a hundred guys back to back in handball. I feel like I just three-sixty-dunked on someone.

Ava soft-smacks me.

WHAT?!

What she smacking me for? Didn't she hear me? Mike came in here bullying me.

"You mad at *me* because I defend myself? I finally fought back," I yell. "Look at *my* face! He smacked the crap out of me!"

Ava rushes to the window.

I follow her fast.

We see him about to turn the corner when he looks up at our apartment and yells, "WATCH! I'm gonna get my boys and we gonna body you!"

He turns and disappears.

• • •

"You dumb!" Ava yells at me. "You know he has a lot of troublemaker friends! Look at what you did! Now he's probably telling them and they're getting yeasted up to fight you."

Right after beating Mike's butt, I felt like that song "All the Way Up" with Fat Joe, Remy Ma, and French Montana. But now Ava just mentioned his homeboys, and my mood's like an elevator and she pushed *B* for basement. I feel the opposite: "All the Way Down."

I try explaining to Ava. "But he disrespected me! He smacked me over and over! What am I supposed to do? I can't let him just smack me! Next thing you know, he'll tell everyone that I'm soft. Then they'll be smacking me. He even said he'd tell Christian to—"

"Okay, okay, but shut up for now!" Ava claps and eyes me in a protective way.

For the first time, I realize she smacked me because she loves me and tried to calm me down.

"So, now what?" she asks. "Mike gets his friends involved. Then, you know Pa's friends are getting involved because they won't let anyone hurt you. Then what happens next? Ugh! I'm going after him."

"What for?"

"To stop him."

CHAPTER 37

Every five minutes after Ava went chasing after Mike, I check the time.

While waiting for her to come home, I feel different feelings.

I feel proud I stood up to him.

I have no doubt that I can kick his butt if he ever tries to one-on-one fight me again.

But I feel another way too. Even though I feel invincible and unbreakable, I don't feel like I can't be hurt. Because I can't fight all the guys he knows. And what if Pa's friends get involved and one of them gets hurt or locked up over me?

Ava is gone, and I go into the bathroom and squint at my fists. My knuckles are red, and my wrists hurt from hitting Mike.

I wipe sweat and tears from my face.

I feel ashamed too.

I don't know why, but I feel that.

• • •

When keys jingle outside our apartment door, I stand at the dinner table.

Ma, Pa, and Ava walk in together, and I freeze.

Ma's and Pa's faces. They *know*.

Pa jokes with Ava and Ma. "I told you Bryan has my temper."

What? He's not mad at me?

He comes, rubs my head like he's proud, then leaves for his and Ma's room.

I start feeling good until I see Ma's tight face. She slides a chair in front of me, sits, and wants to know everything.

Ava stays standing behind her.

"Mike has everyone thinking he's a good kid," I whisper to Ma. "He's not. And he's definitely not my brother. He's not even a friend."

Ava jumps in. "Ma wants to know about the fight, Bryan."

I stare at my red knuckles, then glare at Ava.

Ma tells her, "Ava, leave." She doesn't want to but bounces.

"So, what happened?" Ma asks. "I need you to tell me everything."

• • •

I tell Ma about times Mike called me soft, ways he took my stuff on the regular, bullied me, pushed Dennis and Christian to fight me.

I leave out other stuff. I don't snitch about hopping subway turnstiles, train-surfing into other neighborhoods, or the cops and Little Kevin. I'm mad at him but I don't want to drag him and get him—and me—in more trouble.

Ma stares real hard and caring like she soaks everything up. When I stop, she looks me in my eyes while nodding over and over. "You're done?"

"I guess."

"Why didn't you tell me this stuff before it got out of hand?"

Hearing that makes me wish I said something sooner.

I grab the Nerf basketball he threatened to take. "He thinks he's a superhero and—"

"What do superheroes have to do with this conversation?"

"Me and him used to say which comic hero we wanted to be. But in real life he's not one. He's a bad guy."

"I'm not on his side but *think*," Ma says. "Ava caught *you* beating him up. Some people might say you're the bad guy."

"I'm not."

"In *his* mind, he might think he's not. Listen, you stayed friends with him this whole time so there must be good in him. And what about the bad? Did you try to speak to him about that?"

"No."

"Were there times you could've not followed him doing bad things?"

"Yeah."

"Why didn't you?"

We sit quiet for a long time.

I think about the rush of train-surfing and how I felt free from all my stress. I think about times I followed him *just because.*

I mutter, "Felt good. For fun. Habit."

"So, you see that you made choices, right? You chose *not* to talk first with him. You chose to follow him when he was making the wrong choices, and then you chose to explode on him."

"I was just handling that like a man. Like Pa." As I say it, I feel like a parrot, just echoing what I was taught. "Soft. I can't be that."

Ma sits for a minute not talking.

She says, "I love your father. There a lot of things I love about him. But I don't love that he follows the wrong friends. I don't love that he doesn't try controlling his temper. I don't like when he explodes on people and uses his hands. That's not tough or smart."

I say, "Yeah, but he can't let people disrespect him. And I can't let people disrespect me."

"You're right. But if you start doing what your father does, then you're going to end up where he ends up. Do you think I want to see you in jail?"

I think about it. I hate when Pa is in jail. I would hate it if Ma ever had to hear that I got locked up. And I don't *really* know what jail is like. But I know I never want to go.

"You have choices," Ma says. "You can choose different re-actions. You can choose your friends, ones with different hab-its and different ideas of fun. Mike isn't the only boy in this neighborhood."

I want to tell her, *I didn't choose Mike. You and Pa chose him for me.* Instead, I say, "I felt like I had to hang out with him or hang out with no one."

"That's not true," Ma says. "That boy Will. Julianne and Juan's son. He seems like a nice kid. Why didn't you hang out with him more?"

"I will. I was thinking that the other day when me and him

were in your office. I was realizing he's cool and more my style than Mike. I'm definitely hanging out with him and kids like him more."

I hold up my Nerf basketball. "Mike wanted to take this." I grab my comic. "And this too." I start getting hyped thinking of how he acted then. "You see what I mean by he takes what's mine?"

"Why are we going back to that? Calm down."

"I don't want to see him ever again."

"You're going to see him."

"Why?"

She points at our window. "Because his apartment building is right across from ours. You go to the same school."

"Why'd you even invite him over for dinner that first time?"

Ma lets out a long sigh. "I'm going to tell you something you can't tell Mike."

I wiggle to the edge of my seat. "Okay."

"He came in that day to say there was no food in his refrigerator and that he was hungry."

Ma doesn't know that I already know his fridge stays empty.

She keeps on. "When he told me that, I invited him to dinner. I figured it was safe to have him around you. Because I knew from his mother that his grades showed he was smart and seemed to be going in the right direction."

Then Ma goes into community center mode, explaining how people who have more should do more to help people who have less.

I don't get that because we don't have more than a lot of people.

Ma keeps on, using big words like *obligation, commitment, selflessness,* and *blah-blah-blah.*

I start zoning out and not listening

Then she interrupts me spacing out by flipping it on me and asking if I can have an honest conversation with Mike and make things better.

I ask back, "After everything he did?"

"Especially after everything he did." Ma stares at me serious, leans forward, and rests her hand on mine. "Bryan, I'm not saying you have to go back to being best friends with him. I'm not even saying you should be friends with him. But you need to make this right with him. You and him have history. And you can't walk around with a neighbor who wants to fight you, especially when you know some of his friends are troublemakers. And who knows? Someday, you might need his help."

I suck my teeth. I remember Ava saying that.

Ma stands. "You and him need to talk this out."

"How? I'm not going up to him. If he's still mad, that'll be a fight."

"You're lucky you have Ava," she says. "She got to Mike before he told his friends. She made him promise not to do anything."

"It worked?"

"Well, it helped that Ava made Mike start using his brain

again. She told him to think a few steps ahead to when Pa gets involved. She knows Mike would want to avoid that. So that helped make him promise to talk to you."

Ma goes to leave. "Maybe thank her. And this conversation isn't over. Think about what I said until we talk again."

• • •

Later, dinner is wild. As Pa eats, he eyes me a few times and winks. At one point, he gives me a thumbs-up. Before he went back to jail, he told me don't be soft. Now that I beat up Mike, I guess he knows I'm not and he's proud. Each time he winked at me, I felt like the man, but then I'd look over at Ma and Ava and their expressions said, "What're you smiling for? Stop smiling."

Pa finishes dinner first and tells me, "Bryan, do dishes with me."

Okayeee then. I never do dishes with Pa. This feels a little awkward and I wonder why he's asking.

Me and Pa go in the kitchen.

Pa says, "I wash, you dry," as he hands me a dish towel. "Remember when I told you don't surround yourself with the wrong friends?"

"Yeah."

He turns on the water. "I didn't know Mike was like that, and I'm glad you put him in his place. Before he could hurt you more."

A part of me is proud that Pa is taking my side instead of Mike's. Before, I was afraid to tell Pa that Mike was maybe not a real friend because I was afraid that he thought Mike was the best thing ever. Pa keeps washing dishes and handing me one after the other. He becomes his quiet, non-chatty self, but these minutes together feel good with us doing something together.

• • •

Alone, back in my room, I think about what Ma said about choosing better friends and making things better with Mike.

I go to my comics and flip through the stack while splitting them into piles. I have three *Batmans*, two *Black Panthers*, one *Spider-Man*, and two *Luke Cages*. Seeing the *Batmans*, *Black Panthers*, and *Luke Cages* makes me think back to when me and Mike first met.

Back then, he asked me which superpower I wanted.

I told him Batman's and Black Panther's because they figure out stuff mad fast and know what's happening ten steps ahead. He chose Luke Cage because he's so strong and nothing hurts him.

Right now, I lay a *Luke Cage* comic in between a *Batman* and a *Black Panther* comic. I wonder who would win a fight? Luke Cage or Batman? Luke Cage or Black Panther?

When I fought Mike, I felt like Luke Cage. But what good did being stronger than Mike do? I wasn't thinking. I was just swinging. That made things worse.

If I were Batman or Black Panther, I definitely wouldn't have first fought with my hands. I would've first fought with my head and thought ten steps ahead. If I had, I would've known Mike's next step would be to get revenge by telling his friends.

Luke Cage is the man, but being him with Mike doesn't help. And the truth is, I'm not Luke Cage. Heads can get at me and hurt me. I can bleed.

I need to think with my head.

I lie in bed, put my comics next to me, and look at the ceiling.

Sounds come from outside my window: laughter, music, arguments, and curses. I listen harder at the cursing and arguing. It sounds like a fight might happen any minute. That's every day out here. I make a wish.

I wish things could be different.

Then I remember.

Way back in the day, I made that same wish standing outside the bodega on Pa's corner. I remember wishing I had a brother too. Then life did get different. And I got Mike, who called me a *brother*. Way before those wishes, I remember wishing that my real brothers from Pa would come and teach me brotherly things. I wonder if having Mike is like having a real brother— the good and the bad—because he ended up teaching me stuff. Then again, he would flip and act grimy, cocky, and front with me. I don't know.

I think about Big Will and how he brings only good and no bad. I think about how he's to me what I'm to him: a straight-up friend with no drama. But thinking about him makes me think of something else: advice he gave me. When me and him caught Mike eyeing me all jealous, he said I should talk to Mike to stop his mood from growing into a problem. I should've listened because now me and Mike have a big problem. Come to think of it, Ava told me the same thing Big Will did.

I remember watching her show with her, and right now I hear her in my head, like she's in front of me, saying, ". . . always use your head . . . just because people bug out doesn't make them all bad . . . always talk it out if you can."

I roll over and look at my *Batman* and *Black Panther* comics. They think ten steps ahead. Plus, Ava and Big Will say do that.

Tomorrow . . .

Tomorrow, I *will* dead this drama.

Tomorrow. And forever.

I definitely will use my head.

ACKNOWLEDGMENTS

We need people to keep us going. Charlotte, thanks for that and more. Nancy, thanks for being here for me, great to me, and showing me what to build and add. Thanks, Stacey, for sharing lenses during *Secret Saturdays* that helped me write *Tight*. Jackie, a big thanks for all you've done for me. As always, thanks, Ma, for cheerleading my writing since I was a tot crayoning the alphabet. You're my friend and amazingly more. My wife and daughter: I love you and you help make my writing better and possible. Also, family—blood and in-laws—who loved and supported me at needed times. Thanks to my first readers—my wife and Mark Zustovich. And readers of my unpublished works: Jill Eisenhard and Ebony Wilkins—you helped clear my mind for *Tight* to come through. And thanks to those with writing advice and encouragement from my first book to *Tight*: Marco A. Carrión, Jennifer Clark, Lisa Dolan, Denise Bolds, Ronnie Aroesty, Maurice Mosley, Melissa Archer, and Matt Bird. "It takes a village" and sometimes people don't know their impact: Michael Fraher, Melissa Jacobs,

Paula Madison, Ashindi Maxton, Kalisha Dessources, Eric Luper, Eric Velazquez, and Rebecca Fitting. And thanks to fans of my first book who wanted another. And my students, who inspire me. Together, all of you created experiences and energy that encouraged *Tight* to come into the world.